PRAIRIE SOUL PRESS
Copyright © 2024 Prairie Soul, Inc.

All rights reserved. No part of this publication may be reproduced, distributed, or transmitted in any form or by any means, including photocopying, recording, or other electronic or mechanical methods, without the prior written permission of the publisher, except in the case of brief quotations embodied in critical reviews and certain other non-commercial uses permitted by copyright law.

Individual copyrights on page 135

ISBN-13: 978-1-998232-08-6

GOBLINCORE

(an anthology)

Contents

Goblincore, Lofi & the Folk Tradition............................ 1

In the Hollow ... Cordelia Kelly....................... 7

The Dragonfly ... Margaret Campbell.......................... 13

Mudge ... Kim Claussen................................. 17

Rust for Rot ... Lareina Abbot......................... 23

The Little Mushroom Girl ... Calvin D. Jim 29

Ruby Tips to Her Feathers ... Ash Vale 35

The Crone ... J.A. Renwick............................ 41

Persephone, Queen of—I Don't Know—Some Bugs ... Alex Benarzi 47

The Moon & the Stars ... Joseph Halden & Rhonda Parrish 53

Extinction Burst ... Robert Fields Byrne....................... 59

Forest Magic ... Valerie Hunter....................... 65

A Mountain's Plea ... A.J. McCutchen 71
Roadkill Rising ... Brent Nichols 75
The Eerie Wood ... Emily A. Grigsby 81
The Intelligence ... paulo da costa 89
The Surprise Entrant ... Arvee Fantilagan 93
Amber and Jet ... Christa Bedwin 97
No Matter the Cost ... Meghan Victoria 103
Dirty Girl ... Sarah L. Pratt 109
Sacrifices ... Jason Ellis 117
Seasons ... Nik Kuipers 123
About the Authors 127
Copyrights 135
More 139

Goblincore, Lofi & the Folk Tradition

There's something transgressive about the Goblincore aesthetic. Honestly, in our modern world, any lifestyle that promotes nature, do-it-yourself-ism and going your own way will always be at odds with $12 coffees, software subscription models and LinkedIn hustle culture. Any lifestyle that looks back to the ways most humans lived before the end of the Second World War will be transgressive.

I've always been a sucker for a "it used to be like this before we ruined it" mindset. It's what drew me to folk music and rural blues when I was fifteen. Here was this un-gate-kept (allegedly), DIY music made by people for themselves. There's something very goblin-y about people *producing* their art, not simply consuming it. Screw the system! We can entertain ourselves.

My (late to the party) discovery of Goblincore coincided with long walks listening to lofi. The crackly vinyl effects, the slow BPM and those delicious major seventh chords…it all felt so *healing*. This was music I could enjoy without analyzing it. Without *worrying* about it. Music for the sake of music.

And, like the originators of the folk music I'd fallen in love with so early, it's easily created by people who just love doing it. Screw the system! We can entertain ourselves.

I find both these DIY angles—the folk tradition and lofi—are beautifully expressed in the Goblincore aesthetic. Which brings us to this book.

Why did I put this book together? That's a story. Hope you're sitting comfortably.

After a couple intense years and a deep, deep burnout that I still needed to work and parent through—I can't go on, I'll go on—a long-held backburner suspicion came to the front, and I realized why I'd always had such a hard time in this crazy world of ours—why I'd always felt I was swimming upstream.

Recognizing my neurodivergence led me down a thorny, backwoods path of discovery, leading me to find that, most of all, I needed *rest*. This was no surprise, but the realization convinced me to let myself have that rest.

And I vegged out. Slumped on the couch, scrolling Reddit for hours was exactly what my rat-bite frayed nervous system needed to get enough strength back to become a functional parent, husband and business owner—more than just the ragged remnants of the mask I'd been wearing.

It was here I found the r/goblincore subreddit.

These pictures of moss and mushrooms, animal skulls and snails were somehow soothing, the lines of nature rendered in pixels on a screen still having some of their healing power.

As the snow melted and the rains let up, I started wandering in the provincial park not a ten-minute walk from where I live, but where my previous exhaustion had kept me from. A park I'd wandered through much of my childhood and adolescence.

This reconnecting with nature reconnected me with my own nature, as well. I felt as if I'd come home—come home to a self that had been waiting patiently for me, but which I'd abandoned long ago.

I wanted more of that feeling.

And, as a publisher, what better way to keep a feeling than to put out a call for submissions? I asked for stories based in nature of outsiders coming to find—or create—a home. I encouraged stories from traditional outsider group perspectives, like neurodivergence, BIPOC and LGBTQ+.

And the stories I got were beyond what I could have hoped for. We got 55 submissions for 13 slots! With so many quality submissions, I needed to expand the book to 21 stories. Even then, I had to make some very hard decisions.

So, in this world of generative AI and Instagram filters, please enjoy this folky, lofi collection of outsiders and weirdos, who, in the course of just doing their thing, find solace from a cacophonous world.

(And, if you're looking for some mood music to keep the goblin vibes going, may I present to you the musical composition inspired by these exquisite stories. Scan the code on the next page to choose your preferred music streaming platform).

Yours in all things decaying and green,

jim jackson
founder, editor and wisdom farmer at Prairie Soul Press

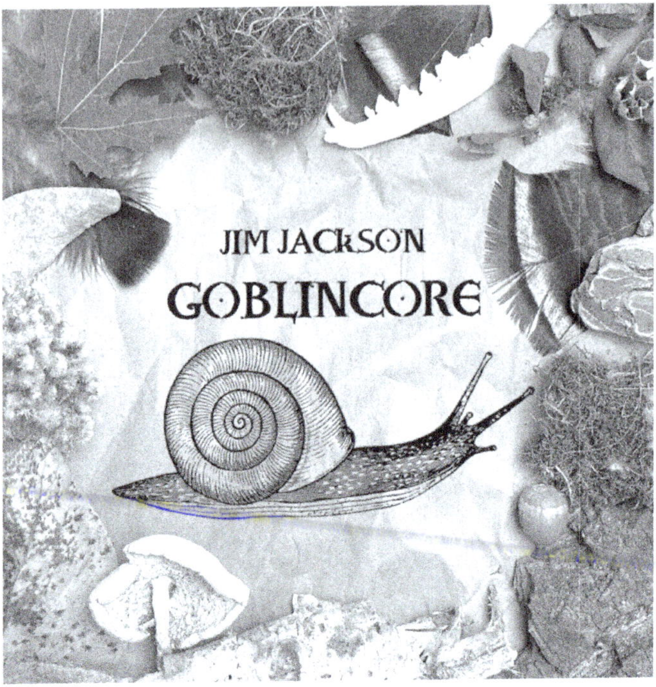
JIM JACKSON
GOBLINCORE

GOBLINCORE

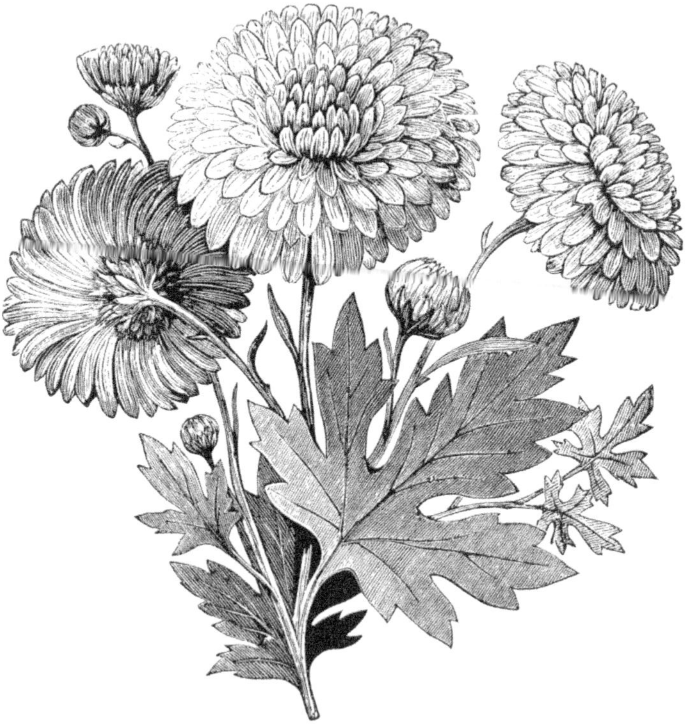

In the Hollow
... Cordelia Kelly

Though the forest was gloomy and let in little light, it never scared Hazel. She had never been the type to discriminate against tutus, but most of the time she wore her jeans ragged and flecked with mud; it was easier to navigate the woods.

Leaving the sunshine and her father's angry growls behind her, she eased over the threshold of the treeline where things were dark and hushed. She paused until her heart stopped racing, breathing in the scent of cedar, mushrooms, and decaying leaves. At ten years old, it was as good of a perfume as Hazel could think of.

She descended the slope to the boggy grounds surrounding the creek. Here, in a hidden hollow, was the best part of the forest, where the ground squelched spongy mud under her sneakers and there was always something new to find. The cool air dried the tears on her cheeks.

A flash of crimson caught her eye. Hazel squatted to eye level with a cluster of mushrooms, standing out like poisonous jewels on a toppled log. The most perfectly formed toadstool she'd ever seen had been broken and listed to the side at the centre.

"What a shame," she muttered, and righted it.

A chittering sounded from the log, different from the muted eerie rustling and dripping down here in the valley. A knot formed in Hazel's stomach as she cast a glance around her, getting the sense she was being watched.

As she braced a hand on the log, ready to flee, she noticed something out of place in the cleft on the log in front of the toadstools.

An acorn, shiny and perfect, was displayed on the mossy wood. No oak trees grew in this part of the forest, and she was sure the acorn had not been there when she arrived.

It had the feel of a gift; something left just for her. Tentatively, she took it with her chipped-paint nails. "Thank you," she whispered. A faint chittering answered her.

On impulse, Hazel unwound the ribbon from her hair, one of her favourites: navy blue, with a spray of sparkles like the night sky. She placed it where the acorn had been and slowly backed away.

The next morning, she returned to the hollow by the creek. The refreshing air cooled her flushed cheeks as she fled from her home, the stinging rebuke from her father ringing in her ears. Here, out of the sunshine, all was serene; the stringent smell of herbs and sap lingered in the air like a tonic to her spirit.

Sitting in the cleft where she'd left her ribbon, surrounded by toadstools like ornaments, was a snail shell.

"How beautiful," she murmured as she lifted it with gentle fingers. The delicate spirals were banded with yellow and brown, the ridges cool and smooth under her fingertips. The inside was empty but slick with slime, as though someone had recently sucked the living occupant out of it.

"Thank you," she said, certain *something* was with her by the log. The chittering came again, like a conversation.

She spent a good part of the day in the hollow. Her stomach clenched from hunger; she hadn't eaten since the night before, but she'd prefer to stay right where she was. It wasn't until late afternoon she heard the shrill edge of her mother's voice, calling her in like a warning.

Dread flooded through her and Hazel jumped up, mud crusting her arms, hair pushed back in sweaty knots. Heart beating to break her chest, she jammed her hand into her pocket and came up with a shiny penny.

"I know this isn't worth very much," she said in a breathless rush. "But it's my lucky penny. I found it at the fair and then won a prize, so that's got to mean something. I hope it brings you luck, too."

She placed it with care in the dip on the log, nestled in moss. A hissing came from under the log, and all the hair on her neck prickled, but not in a frightening way. Whatever lay under the log, she knew plenty scarier things.

She scrambled up the slippery ravine, out of the bog and on her way home.

It was three days before Hazel came back to the log. She bore a paper sack in her arms and a bright band of slapped swollen skin on her cheek. "I brought my lunch," she told the log without preamble. "I don't have much, but I can share."

She laid half of her limp ham sandwich on the log and sat back, resting her legs and chewed the rest of the sandwich. Her blood still pounded from when she'd left her house, but eventually, the peace of the hollow found its way inside of her and she let her eyes drift shut. If only she could find herself a patch of moss to make her bed and live here with the forest creatures.

Or better yet, if only Hazel could make herself a tree, a girl of bark and sap and twigs; no one could ever hurt her.

She opened her eyes and the sandwich on the log was gone. In its place was a skull.

The pointed muzzle and large front teeth told her it was a rodent; she'd guess a squirrel based on the size. The bone had been polished until it gleamed dully. She picked it up and rotated it, inspecting every aspect.

"It's perfect." Her voice was a reverent whisper.

Too late she heard the footsteps crashing towards her.

"Here you are!" Her father's boots squelched into the mud. "This is where you spend your days, getting filthy and avoiding your chores? What a waste of space you are." He hauled Hazel up by her arm. She cried out as the skull went flying from her hand, back into the bog where it would probably be safer.

"Dad! I was just—" But there wasn't anything to say to dissolve the rage that pulsed behind his eyes. It always lurked there, sometimes more present than others, but nothing could make it go away completely.

"Just what? Just hanging out in the mud. No wonder you have no friends. This place is disgusting, like you." He wound himself up and kicked the crimson toadstools right off the log.

"No, you can't!" Hazel screamed as the chittering sounded, loud and frantic, building up into a roar that overtook everything in the woods. It was like the thunder of a flooding river, all mud and violence and crashing destruction.

"What the—" Her dad peered around the hollow, not understanding the danger.

A hole appeared in the log, once hidden by the cluster of mushrooms, opening to darkness. It stretched out like a gaping maw, and something about it made Hazel want to cover her eyes, cover her ears against the mudslide of rage. She backed away until her sneakers sank entirely into the boggy mud.

They glittered like onyx as they came, a swarm of beetles with shimmering carapaces. They poured out of the mouth of the rotting log, more and more and more as though they came from a deep hole underneath, one that went down into the earth, filled with pincers and clicking wings and chittering.

The insects reached her father's boot and didn't stop, climbing faster than she thought possible as they overtook him. At first, he tried to pull them off; at first, he tried to run. Then he tried to scream, until he could no longer do that.

Hazel cowered in the mud. Finally, the chittering stopped and, like a sunbeam that comes out from behind a cloud, the hollow seemed to lighten. She looked up, slowly. Stretched out in front of the log was a skeleton, gleaming dully in the dim light. Already it was sinking into the bog.

Hazel straightened, wary of beetles, but there were none to be seen. She took in a hitching breath. "I think…I think this is a gift best left hidden," she said. The gaping mouth on the log already sprouted minute crimson toadstools, like bloody teeth. She stumbled away, squelching through the mud, away from the log.

She would never return to this part of the woods.

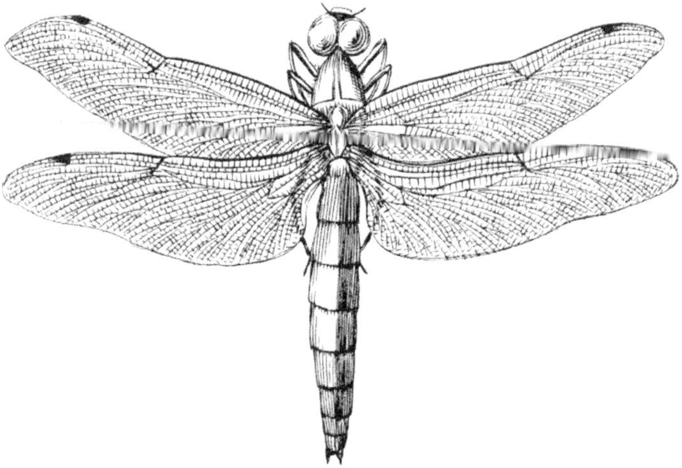

The Dragonfly
... Margaret Campbell

She was once one sort of witch and is now another. Couldn't the same be said of you, whatever you are? When she built the stone cottage, she built it with her own two hands (which *apparently* must be said, and not by devils contracted with acts of sexual congress, though that would have been her own business and exceedingly pragmatic besides) and at that time she was fat and strong, not still young nor yet old. She built it on the precipice between two states of being, the segue between one life and another.

Her first magic, long before the cottage, had been the unwitting magic of innocence. To the flowers, into the soft furls of their petals, as soft as her small and dimpled hands, she whispered her kindly little dreams. The flowers kept them at the petals' white roots, the anchor between petal and stem. The flowers knew her, then, would infinitesimally turn their heads to her, and sometimes granted her most insubstantial wishes; flowers, you see, for all their best intentions, are very poor wish-granters. Bees carried the dreams from one flower to another, back again, toddering through the air, weighed down with pollen and sweet magic, delicate legs dripping with the dew of gentle dreams. But no dreamer is gentle forever.

A dragonfly once heard a father whisper with a wink to a small girl, even smaller than the witch was then, that if the dragonfly flew too close, it would sew her mouth shut. The dragonfly, not understanding the intricacies of winks and knowing even less of the strange mischief of fathers, flew with a cruel new iridescence on its wings, the blue sheen of menace. And so, after the flowers had turned from the young witch, after her dreams had become too heavy for them to properly hold, too strange to cling to the bees, it was the dragonfly who found them.

In pursuit of a midge one afternoon, the dragonfly lit upon a flower which was looking rather poorly, hanging its sallow pink head. A dragonfly has no particular business with the flowers and only ever carries pollen from one to another by accident, often in the act of hunting the sweet-legged and toddering bees. But immediately upon landing the dragonfly noticed the dark luster of a strange and twisting dream. It was odd; flowers never held such magic. On a whim, the dragonfly took the dream along with it. The dream spread along its hunting path through the forest, to a vine of ivy and a stand of rowan, to a rosemary bush and thistles and belladonna. These all held a dark dream well. They grew with the dream, around it, and this was its own sort of magic. Later, the witch would see her dreams in them, would know immediately by sight or touch or smell just what magic each would produce. This was a much more efficacious gift than small wishes, feebly granted.

The thought of her cottage out in the forest, past the edge of her little village, among the ivy and the rowan, was conceived when the witch tired of neighbors. She had long grown tired of whispers, and even longer tired of people who wanted to *pop in*, that was how they always put it, crying *just curious*, pawing through her glass jars of toad livers, her delicate clumps of herb tied with twine. They wanted nothing to do with her, or even with her magic, except to see it so they could go out and tell their friends how strange and uncouth it all was. How many eyeballs looked out at them from her shelves, how potent the smell of drying bones, how frightening, how odd. Warn their wives off coming around, tout the wholesomeness of the doctor, with his scientific mind and his gleaming surgical instruments.

So she went to live past the brambles and the beginnings of forest. She cleaved open trees, and blessed their hearts, and used them for timber-frame construction. She harvested the stone herself and learned to read its grain (which is not unlike reading tea leaves, really), and chiseled it to bricks. She built all the walls with small openings under the eaves, for ventilation in the summer, you understand. When the wind blew through them, they did make a low sort of wailing sound, oft heard by busybody passersby. She loved how it warned them off. She laughed her hearty laugh over the wailing. Carried on the wind, through the eaves, it may have sounded something like a cackle.

She ate mainly berries, and roasted chestnuts, and the bits of small animals that were no good for doing any magic with, and she grew thin and her hair gray. It was around then that she became less a member of the community than one of its myths, one of the things you scare the children with. *You see that dragonfly? Don't let it get too close, it'll sew your mouth right shut. You see that cottage, there, through the trees?*

None who enter leaves—the witch uses their organs for magic, and the rest for stew.

And yet, even then, reduced and inflated to monstrosity, the witch would never really be left alone. Among those who came to her for more than morbid curiosity, there had always been the desperate. She was happy to weed out all but them. Though she was not quite happy, per se, to see their eyes flash wildly with fear when they entered the cottage, always late at night, with their tear-streaked faces and their mud-laced skirts. Their fears always faded fast; a thin old witch never held a candle to their own nightmares. It was only with the desperate that she recollected her gentle dreams. They told her theirs, how they had twisted, what cast shadows upon them. The witch held it all, and she granted their wishes with a vengeance.

Mudge
... kim Claussen

All his life, Mudge wanted to be a different kind of jeeb. (Granted, his life so far had been about one and a half seasons in the forest of Yhdessä, but still).

He wasn't like the water jeebs. They were graceful and smooth, flowing over creek stones, bubbling around fallen branches. They twisted with ease, swirling and fluid. They splashed and played and swam with each other, languid and smiling.

He wasn't like the fire jeebs, either. They were bright, crackling with energy and heat. They jittered over the ground, leaving bold trails for others to try to follow. When they clapped, sprinkles of sparks fluttered up towards the sky.

He wasn't even like the air jeebs—though that one, he didn't mind so much. The air jeebs were, well, flighty. They liked to be extremely high up, where they did their cloud weaving, or dip down to tickle the tops of trees. Sometimes they would fly down when the sky was gray, so they could dance (or fight) with the water jeebs. At least, it looked like fighting because of all the crashing noise and flaring shocks of light, but they never seemed angry after, just refreshed.

No, Mudge wasn't like any of the other jeebs.

🍄

When Mudge tried to run and jump like Ember, he thumped instead.

"Like this," Ember would say, skipping over the grass, leaving sparks and wafting trails of smoke in her wake. "It's easy!"

Mudge screwed up his face and tried to do what she did. Instead, he rolled, bonking his mossy head against the ground. He tipped this way and that, landing with a thud and a creaky, scraping sigh.

Ember laughed, a loud snapping sound. "You're so weird."

🍄

Mudge thought maybe he was better suited to being a water jeeb (he was hard like the stones in the creek, so this made sense. Plus, the creek was a cool relief from the heat).

Until he tried to *be* a water jeeb.

Dewy shaped himself around sticks and stones in the creek, slipping and gliding against its banks, smooth and simple. Mudge took a deep breath and jumped over the bank to mimic his movements. But Mudge got wedged between a cluster of twigs until Dewy shoved him through. Mudge banged and bounced against sand and stones, ungainly and awkward.

Then he sank—straight down to the muddy creek bed. This was when he discovered that he was *much* heavier than the water jeebs, and his arms and legs were much too short for swimming.

Mudge groaned, his insides hard and hot with embarrassment when Dewy and seven other water jeebs had to push him into the shallows so he could climb out. He sat on the grassy edges of the creek, watching the water jeebs play and babble.

"You'll get it someday," Dewy soothed, arms swishing.

Dewy's big misty hair made Mudge's scrubby face moist. Mudge was grateful—no one could tell what was mist and what wasn't. Dewy pretended not to notice Mudge's sniffling.

🍄

The only things Mudge seemed to be good at were rolling and sitting, which, in his opinion, were extremely un-jeeb-like. And sometimes he wasn't even very good at rolling.

He reached a hill and went too fast down the other side. He flattened mushrooms, he whacked against tree trunks. So, he rolled home, his insides hard and hot with embarrassment again.

"You'll find your way." Mama patted his mossy head with her little paws.

Mudge said nothing. He wanted to believe her; he loved her very much. But Mama wasn't a jeeb—she was a brown mouse who had found an abandoned pebble one day and brought it home.

🍄

As winter crept over the forest, things became distinctly different, besides the air being (pleasantly) cold. The water jeebs grew sleepy and were no longer as playful. They stretched out, becoming as stiff as Mudge was; some of them grew crystals on their nose and ears. Gone were their graceful flowing movements—instead, they were either clonky like him, or they didn't bother to move much at all. Dewy didn't like the cracks that formed on his face.

"I can't wait for spring," he sighed, like a fine, cool fog. "Being stuck is *so* boring."

The fire jeebs were even more irritated by winter. They huddled together in pockets of sheltered soil and ignored everyone else, complaining about the chilly air and the crust of frost coating the ground and trees. When it came, they hated the snow that coated the forest floor, too—refusing to venture over the crisp white surface.

"Ugh, I want the dry heat of summer back." Ember flickered and frowned, trying to fan her hair higher but it stubbornly lay in limp, smoky tendrils.

Mudge tried hard not to smile. For once, being the weird jeeb didn't feel so bad.

He had nearly no problems in winter at all. He could stand on top of the snow or cozily nap underneath it. He could cross the creek without sinking. He could roll and zig-zag (if not quite jump) like Ember without getting tangled in tall grass. He could even bumble over the hills with more control, as the snow helped him move a little slower, sink in a little bit, steer better.

Being the only jeeb out and about was strangely freeing—he could roll anywhere he wanted without feeling like he was doing something wrong. Being the only jeeb moving amongst the trees was fun.

At first.

It soon became very, very lonely.

The air jeebs stayed up high in the sky, hardly coming down. Sometimes they blustered and spun through when it snowed, but they always seemed in such a hurry to go somewhere else and didn't stop to talk. Sometimes they were downright icy, blasting the snow around to create piles and drifts, ignorant of everyone else's discomfort. Mostly though, they erased the prints and paths he'd made all over the forest floor before then they dashed back up to the clouds. The next day he got to roll over fresh powdery snow to make new paths—so sometimes, it wasn't so bad. But even this was only fun so many times before it, too, was very, very lonely.

Because there was only one path in the white. Just his.

There was none of Dewy's mist to hide the moisture that kept gathering on Mudge's face, which the cold turned into glittering frost. Mama nested during the day and nipped out at night to search for nuts and seeds for herself. Mudge, being a jeeb, didn't eat, so he stayed behind and tried to ignore the cold ache inside him that was altogether quite separate from the cold of winter.

His loneliness only grew when Mama stopped coming back home one long autumn. This was sometimes the way of the other animals in the forest, but it didn't stop him from feeling deeply terrible inside.

With Mama gone, the first tendrils of chilly winter wind beckoned Mudge to explore.

This time, he went farther than he'd ever gone before. Mudge rolled, leaving uneven tracks in the snow as usual, and he tumbled all the way to the edge of the forest...

Then beyond.

Through deeper snow, he bumbled and climbed. A large dark shape loomed up, so high that the top of it was lost somewhere amongst the air jeebs and their clouds. Mudge stared. It was sort of like a creek stone, but impossibly huge. And there was no creek and no water jeebs in sight. Trees peppered up its sides, snow draped down it. It seemed to go on forever.

At the base of the giant rocky stone, something stirred amongst the expanse of white snow. Mudge paused. This was the farthest he'd ever been from home—which had been sort of exciting and exhilarating until *right now*. Now it seemed actually very foolish and completely dangerous.

A set of eyes poked out of the snow.

"Hallo?" came a voice, scraping and rumbly.

Bits of brown moss flaked off the sides of the small rounded shape as it poked up higher.

Mudge stayed still, pretending to be invisible like an air jeeb.

"Granite? Wake up, we have a visitor."

He'd never been good at being at an air jeeb.

And then more shapes stirred in the snow. Mudge had the urge to roll home as fast as he could, but before he could urge himself to action, the shapes... *rolled* to *him*. They clonked and bonked, making jagged paths and trenches in the snow. There were a dozen of them—some of them were Mudge-grey, some of them were more black or more brown or had colorful lines and cracks streaking through their craggy, uneven features.

"Oh!" the one in the front blinked at him. "Well, hi there, little one. Welcome home."

And as it turned out, Mudge was *very, very* good at being an earth jeeb.

Rust for Rot
... Lareina Abbot

The Calgary Drop-In Centre was the farthest place you could get from nature. It felt dead, with its brick, worn concrete and steel. It was a roof to cover her, a kitchen to feed her, but it was not a home. Nothing had seemed like home since she'd lost her mom, and her life, in the house fire in their town of Prince George, B.C.

In Prince George, you could see the northern lights from your porch and nature whispered to you out your front door. It was where she saw things she couldn't explain. She had once seen a man turn into an owl. She had seen mushrooms grow overnight in the spot where a woman had died. There was magic of a kind both dark and necessary. She had always felt the magic of places, and so it seemed so wrong to have ended up in a place with none.

The air shimmered with silvery rain as Trina walked out and slipped away from the clot of people at the entrance. She snuck past the tent city that lined the security fence, her heart beating rapidly, and headed down towards the river walkway.

She'd only been in Calgary for two months, but she'd heard enough stories to know that she didn't want to sleep at the Drop-In Centre. She didn't know where she fit into the homeless hierarchy. There were the people who seemed to have been there forever. There were the shouters; the women and men that were always picking a fight. There were the substance users; she didn't blame them really, she also longed for some release. There were people who were down on their luck but who watched out for some of the others, like the old Cree guy that burned sage by the front door. But then there were the tough guys who roughed up whoever they could, who took advantage of the desperate. They rode around on stolen bikes, jeans slung low showing thin wiry frames, she called them the Rust, as their bikes creaked in the rain, and they felt jagged like an old chainsaw. When she first got here, one of them cornered her in a hallway she hadn't known not to walk down, and who knows what would have happened if it weren't for Sasha. Sasha, who had gone missing two days ago. Sasha, tanned and lithe, who also longed for nature, for trees, for a way out.

The deceptively light rain fell in steady drizzle. She glanced back as she walked along the river; if she was going to find a private place to sleep, she had to make sure that no-one was following her.

It didn't help that she was so small. "*My little forest mouse*," her mother used to call her. She went to the Drop-In Centre because it was the only place where she could get a plate of warm food. Since she'd hitchhiked out of PG, she was always hungry, all the time. The spam and beans she'd had for dinner sat heavy in her stomach. For a moment she let herself remember what her mom's meals were like, bannock and stew, homemade burgers, oatmeal and raisins in the morning, but it was too painful, and the memory washed away with the rain. There was no going back.

She walked across the pedestrian bridge that crossed the river and took the side ramp to a long, thin tree-covered island. During the day young families with kids played in the island playground and swam in the shallow pool, but it was evening and there was no one there, having abandoned the island for their warm, well-lit houses. She ducked under the ramp and looked for a dry spot. A dirty concrete block had escaped the drip of rust water from the metal beams above and so she dusted the dirt off with the corner of her sleeve and sat.

Her brown Vans were already wet. Long dark hair hung down the front of her shoulders, descending from her hood like rivulets of ice water on a thawing mountain. The pointed brown cotton hood and jacket was not the warmest thing, but there was no way she'd take it off. Her body ached with a grief no warmth could heal—Sasha had been gone for two days. Something was wrong, she could feel it.

The bridge spanned the Bow River, all modern and concrete and metal. The river rushed on both sides, swollen with the new rain, and for a moment she closed her eyes and let the sound wash over her. The burble calmed her jangly nerves, until the sound of multiple bikes rumbling over the pedestrian walk clanged above her. She jumped up, a group of that many bikes could only mean one thing. She crouched and looked out from under the walkway. She caught her breath as the five wiry men sat on bikes on the path, it was the Rust.

She ducked back and tried to calm her fast breathing. She glanced over again, one of the men pointed under the walkway, and she caught her breath. They all wore white sneakers and hoodies, as city as it gets, but it made it easy to see their movements in the rain. When they turned their bikes her way, she slid over to the other side of the walkway, and when they reached the opening, she scurried out the other side. She was out in the open now, if one of them saw her, she didn't know what would happen. No one was around. Who would care?

She made a soft, quiet beeline for the woods lining the river past the playground. It was fall and the beginnings of the wine and yellow and colours made their ways into the green leaves. She didn't look back, just concentrated on stepping lightly over the crushed rock on the path. One step, then the next, past the tiered sitting area down to the pool, almost at the playground, then past. She stole a look backwards and took her first deep breath as she walked into the wood. She walked farther in, and the trees grew thick. The cottonwoods twisted in a way that seemed to shield her, and she touched the rough bark of one then the other as she made her way down the slope towards the river. Immediately she felt better, and she settled beneath one of them. A calm descended on her, and she felt a comforting presence.

"Sasha?" She whispered.

Nothing.

She looked around, it was like she had discovered a different Calgary. Her back scratched against the tree, and the dry dirt beneath the spreading branches felt nicer than the concrete. Disintegrating copper leaves lined her little spot, and she smelled a soft blanket of mildew as they broke down in the rain. Bright white mushrooms grew out of a fallen tree at her feet, sheltered by an overhang of moss. She had traded rust for rot.

By her feet, a mouse popped out of the fallen log and stood on its haunches. It peered at her, head sideways. She imagined that she looked like part of the tree, with her brown clothing and dirty pants. She smiled. The mouse seemed... familiar.

Then the mouse looked past her, and over her shoulder. She glanced back. One of the men had stopped his bike on the path above her. She held her breath.

No, please no.

"Hey, guys, I think someone's in here." His laugh felt dark and heavy in the rain.

She bowed her head and sent a silent prayer to whatever gods were out here. *Please, please, anything but this. Woods protect me, please.*

She dug her hands into the wet leaves and the soft green moss.

The mouse, still at her feet, ran up beside her, coming close to her hand. She twitched, and it jumped back.

She pulled her knees up to make herself smaller and looked back.

"Ha! I see her!" The man yelled, jumping off his bike.

Please.

And then the mouse bit her. She heard the forest then, suddenly, like it was inside her, filling her head with its sounds. Saliva and blood, mold and mildew, all mixed into one beautiful thing. Sound became bright, and she stopped hurting. Warmth enveloped her in its softness.

🍄

Jared threw his bike down and jumped into the clearing with Duke.

"Where is she?"

"I swear, she was right here! I saw her eyes, all scared."

"Well then where'd she go?"

"Fuck if I know."

"Well, shit."

Jared pushed Duke, who stumbled, swearing. They walked back to the bikes and rode away up the path.

The two mice watched them go. One tan, and one brown. The brown one finished nibbling a seed, her belly full. The tan one turned, and they ran together into a hole in the fallen tree, into the softness of the forest, out of the rain.

She was home.

The Little Mushroom Girl
... Calvin D. Jim

Kinoko examined the few Shiitake mushrooms in her small hands, gazed inside the rectangular basket, and sighed. Only a third full. Not enough to show after hours of foraging in the thick forest. She was far from her farming village and would have to walk even further if she wanted more. With drought decimating the rice crop and Oji-san ill, Oba-san depended on her. They had been so kind to her after her parents died. She couldn't let them down.

She crouched, pulled hemp straps over her shoulders and stood. The straps dug into her skin even through the yukata; the bottom of the basket scraped against the hem of her calf-length blue-striped trousers. "You can't carry that basket," Oba-san chided. "You'd fall over if it were full," Oba-san was always over-protective of her thirteen-year-old niece.

Maybe that's why the other girls were so mean to her. She was just too small. An easy target.

"Mushroom Girl, Mushroom Girl," the girls in the village taunted her as they threw mud at her. "Dirty-faced Mushroom Girl." Kinoko often returned home, her blue trousers and yukata covered in brown smudges. Kinoko was only happy to venture deep into the dense forest accompanied only by the songs of swallows and warblers if only to avoid the mean girls.

Kinoko spied an overgrown path up a mountain, away from the main path. Perhaps there were more tiny prizes near the top, more Shimeji for Oba-san to boil in nabe in winter. She brushed the shrubs aside and started up the path, her mouth watering as she climbed.

As she crested the top of the hill, she spied a weathered, old shrine in a clearing behind a faded torii gate with a broken arch. Kinoko stared at the shrine as she approached the torii. No larger than Oji-san's farmhouse, the shrine's sloping roof and upswept eaves were still intact, but dense brush covered the area where there should be sliding doors.

Oji-san loved taking his niece to the shrines for New Year and other yearly festivals. A sense of calm seemed to ripple through her as she approached. Kinoko's face brushed against sticky, fibrous strands. A spider web.

"Yuck."

Kinoko squeezed her eyes shut flailing wildly at the webs stretching across her face with her hands, blindly walking toward the shrine. The webs clung to her hair, her clothes, strands sticking stubbornly to her fingers, unable to shake them off. She felt enveloped in webs, trapped and unable to move.

And where was the spider?

She shuddered, opening her eyes, her gaze darted around her body, brushing it frantically with still-sticky hands, her heart racing as Kinoko tried to find the hunter at the heart of the web, to avoid its sting.

Kinoko saw something move near the torii's pillars and turned to gaze at a spider hanging from a long silken strand. Its body and outstretched legs larger than the palm of her hand. Its long abdomen an iridescent blue with yellow stripes and bright red accents. Its spindle legs dark blue with the same yellow stripes at each joint.

It was beautiful. Like a shimmering jewel.

Kinoko could not avert her gaze from the spider as it descended silently to the ground. It scuttled toward her. Kinoko pulled back from it until it stopped and scuttled back, its fanged head always facing her.

Then she noticed several Shiitake on the ground. They must have fallen from her basket while she scrambled through the spider webs. She began picking them up when she noticed the spider scuttling toward her, a mushroom in a web behind it, as if dragging prey.

Kinoko picked up the mushroom and brushed the strands off it. "Thank you," she said bowing slightly. Wait. Was she seriously bowing toward a spider?

The yellow-striped spider scuttled toward the dilapidated shrine and Kinoko followed. She gazed up toward the shrine's ceiling and gasped. Clusters of webs so thick, she almost mistook them for clouds lined the ceiling. And inside them, hundreds of blue and yellow striped spiders scuttled inside them.

Kinoko walked into the village and before she had even gotten home, the girls were already hurling insults at her. Kinoko seethed but ignored them and hurried home.

When she walked through the door, Oji-san was lying by the hearth, Oba-san hunched over him. She leapt up and hugged her niece.

"Where have you been?" said Oba-san holding back tears. "You've been gone for a week. We were worried sick."

Up until now, Kinoko had never been gone foraging for more than a few hours.

Kinoko took the basket off her back and opened it up. Inside, the basket was full of mushrooms of every variety.

Oba-san rooted through them and lifted a long, thick mushroom with a small cap and sniffed it. "Matsutake?"

Kinoko nodded. Matsutake were rare and luxurious. "There's more. A lot more."

"How…?"

"I met a few friends near an abandoned shrine. They helped me."

"Abandoned shrine?" A look of recognition came across Oba-san's face. "Up in the mountains?"

Kinoko nodded.

Oba-san pointed to the white silken pouch tied with a string hung on her shoulders. "And where did you get that?"

"Same friends," said Kinoko.

Oba-san reached for the bag and Kinoko stepped back. Oba-san shook her head, a look of annoyance on her face. She turned and began rooting through the basket. "We can sell the Matsutake and get medicines for Oji-san. He has been sick for days since you left."

But Kinoko was not listening. Instead, she noticed a gossamer web in the corner above a shelf stacked with earthenware bowls. A large spider with a familiar black abdomen and yellow stripes sat in the middle. Waiting for its prey. She walked toward the corner and reached up toward the spider and gently touched the web. The spider scuttled along the web toward her hand and as Kinoko opened her hand, it crawled onto her fingers into her palm.

A hand touched Kinoko's shoulder. Kinoko started.

Kinoko turned toward Oba-san.

"They will never understand," said Oba-san.

"They don't have to."

🍄

Kinoko spent the night helping Oba-san cook a simple stew with some of the Shiitake and nursing Oji-san back to health. The next morning, she left with an empty basket promising to bring back more mushrooms and not to stay away as long.

It was early, but not so early that the village girls weren't out to taunt her.

"Mushroom Girl, Mushroom Girl! Dirty-faced Mushroom Girl."

The first girl had picked up some mud and was getting ready to throw it at her when she noticed the silk pouch hanging from Kinoko's shoulder.

"What's in that?" she said. "Gimme."

Kinoko gave her a wry smile. "Why don't you open it and take it?"

The girl reached out and touched the silk pouch. "Ooo, nice." She said. The girl untied the string holding the pouch closed.

A half-dozen or so spiders crawled out of the pouch. One leapt on the girl's hand and started crawling up her cloth shirt.

The girl screamed, waving her arm to shake the spider off her, but it stuck to her clothes and ran up her neck into her hair. The girl ran, screaming all the way.

The remaining spiders crawled to the ground and toward the other girls. Dozens of other spiders crawled out from the pouch, skittering about on Kinoko's clothes, into the folds of her sleeves, onto her face and into her hair. Kinoko stood there without moving as the spiders crawled everywhere.

The other girls screamed and ran away.

One spider crawled onto her right arm and into her hand. It had a familiar iridescent blue body, yellow stripes and red accents. She gazed at it and smiled. "Thank you," Kinoko said.

As if given a signal, the spiders climbed back into the pouch. Kinoko tied the string and tightened the pouch before starting toward the path that led to the mountain shrine. Villagers pointed at her and gaped, their daughters cowering behind them.

Kinoko smiled. "Let's go home."

Ruby Tips to Her Feathers
... Ash Vale

I am on the hunt for beautiful dead things.

When I meander through these woods, I always look for something unusual, anything precious. My bare feet carry me softly between elms and birch and saskatoons, their berries barely a thought this early in the spring. Today, the prize I seek must be beautiful, but it must also once have been alive and not harmed by my own hand; I require feathers, or fur, or skin.

My love is molting, you see.

Outside her control, her feathers will fall to the ground in clumps, painful nubs left in their stead until regrowth winds its way through her body. It happens with the changing of seasons, like now, when the rotting leaves of winter abandon their decay to make room for new growth. There is magic inherent in transition. Much like the budding blossoms that will soon emerge, my love must shed her snowy plumage in order to usher in her spring skin.

This upheaval leaves her vulnerable to the lingering bite of frost. She requires warmth, and life recently taken, to imbue her with the strength to finish her transformation.

Nothing she gives is wasted. Our children will collect the softness of her plumes and use it to craft clothes, or to fashion masks for each other, or to decorate our hidden home, keep it safe from prying eyes.

The children wish to go into the woods to find what she needs, but this is my duty alone to her, as it always has been. As it always will be.

They groaned and gnashed at me from behind tiny, pointed teeth when I told them they could not follow. I patted their heads, all fur and hide and feathers of their own, and threatened them with hexes I would never cast. I laughed as they shrieked and scattered, leaving behind footprints webbed and cloven alike.

And so I walk, low to the ground, searching for an ensnared jackrabbit or unlucky doe amidst the trees.

That is when I see the girl at the edge of the forest.

🍄

The girl is young, maybe ten summers alive, pink-skinned and child-limbed, fresh from an unknown hurt. She is dressed in fine clothing and wary of me, as she should be. Her long copper hair spirals over the luscious fur of her cloak. I watch her, just as she watches me.

I wait. Finally, she speaks.

"I have been told that a devil woman owns these woods." She clears her throat and stands taller, raising her chin. Her hands tremble. "Are you she?"

I smile sharply and curtsy, holding the rags of my dark clothing out in a mockery of the customs she knows. "I am her."

Her eyes widen and her hand goes inside her cloak to what I assume must be a dagger at her hip, but she does not draw it.

"And do you–do you steal children? As they say?"

I cannot help it–I tip my head back and laugh, loud and long. She takes a step backward, her hand tensing on an unseen hilt. She is brave and reckless, this little one. I like her already.

"No, child, I steal nothing. I take only what comes willingly."

I am not expecting the relief that crests her smooth face. She rubs a small hand at the dark circles beneath her eyes.

"What…what happens to the children? The ones who go with you?"

I consider her. How great her fear must be to seek me out despite the tales she has been told. How great indeed, that she might welcome an unspecified harm over whatever harm she is already familiar with.

"They are given a choice. They can turn back, return to the circumstances from whence they came."

She flinches at this.

"Or, they can be changed, and live forever. But they can never return to what they knew. This is our bargain."

Silent tears fall down her rosy cheeks. She glances behind her, past the edge of the woods where her village must lie. Her eyes track over the fading remnants of snow on the ground, the tall dry weeds poking through, until she turns around and meets my eyes. She gives a short nod, and I beckon for her to follow me. We have a dead thing to find, first.

🍄

A rabbit, recently snared by a hunter nowhere to be seen, is my found offering as I return home. The children are naught but glowing eyes in the dark, wary of the child who follows me. She is exhausted from trudging through the thick, her face still tracked with dirt and tears. Her eyes widen as my partner comes into view. My love is tall beyond even the largest human man, beautiful and terrifying, my magnificent bird-human.

As we walked, the girl explained her plight. She is to be married to a cruel, grey-haired man, already thrice a widower, his other young wives dead in childbirth. The wedding is in two days' time. She is the only daughter, she told me, an excellent trade for power and land, particularly with her unusual red hair.

She shivers now, her eyes watching my partner carefully, the heat from the fire only beginning to stave off the cold the evening brings. I crouch in front of her and take her hands in mine.

"This is your last chance. You can return now, to your mother and father, and forget what you have seen here."

She shakes her head the slightest bit, her curls bouncing.

"Or, you can be changed."

Her trembling has nothing to do with the cold now, I imagine. She nods. I watch her carefully for several seconds more, but I find no hesitation on her face, in her eyes. I stand.

"Very well."

And so, my partner rips the remaining feathers from her back. She leaves broken calamus in her hand's wake, gathers downy love in her palms and presents it to the child, who takes the pale feathers in her small hands. I quickly and deftly skin the rabbit and offer it to my love in return. She accepts it gratefully, along with the peaceful magic from my palms, and begins the process of stretching and fitting it to her form. It will provide her protection until her new feathers grow in.

The girl looks to me, then around the room, to the many small faces of half-children that have emerged to watch the transformation. One steps forward cautiously, a small squirrel-boy. He tilts his head to and fro, observing the girl, who openly returns his observation. The girl grins warmly at him, and I know that it is time.

🍄

My love's feathers have come in again, the tawny brown of spring inviting on her new plumage. I groom her gently as we sit outside in the tall green grasses, awaiting the heat and growth of summer. The children chase each other, shrieking and flapping and crawling around, noisy and joyful. One stops for a moment to watch us; a regal, snowy owl-child with the most beautiful ruby tips to her feathers. She smiles, wild and uninhibited, then runs off to join the others.

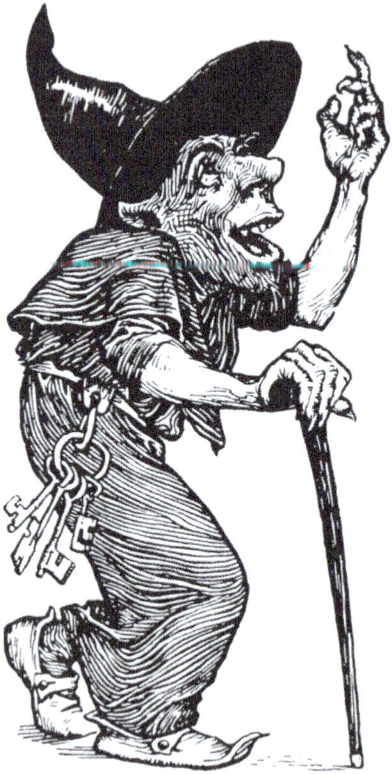

The Crone
... J.A. Renwick

Thorns from the blackberry bushes snag my skirt, clawing at me like the relentless ache in my ribcage. Moonlight filters through the reaching branches above me, their empty bones rattling in the breeze as if in warning. Go back. Keep trying. Avoid the crone at all costs—

my body

my mind

my dignity.

And yet, a yearning tugs me deeper into the midnight forest, where the crone lies waiting. She's been calling to me for months now. With every step I take toward her, the trees grow more withered. More twisted. More hunched with shame. Just like me and my barren womb.

How long have the trees rotted here? Their roots digging further into the soil, like skeletal fingers desperately searching for one last morsel. One last chance at nourishment. A final shot to thrive and do what every living thing is meant to—create life.

Even the simple brown mushrooms lining the trail contain billions of spores. As I kick one, I imagine those spores floating off to settle in warm, damp, safe places, where fresh little mushrooms will flourish.

Me? I have no spores. No warm safe space for new life to grow. Only a hostile cavern with bloody walls and sharp teeth, only good for gnawing at my core. And no matter how much hope, or prayer, or good food, or medicine and surgery, or hormonal injections, or intentions to *just relax*—it only bites harder, tearing at my flesh and my soul.

My toe catches on a root, and I steady myself on a gnarled trunk. My fingers graze its rough surface, finding a round knot. It regards me like a pitying eye, searching for what must be wrong with me. After all, I've been told every woman longs to be a mother and would do anything to become one. They'd walk through fire, letting the flames peel away their skin and the ashes scorch their lungs. It doesn't matter if their charred bodies and minds begin to flake away, as long as they come out the other side holding a baby with healthy smooth skin and bright curious eyes. Or at least, they'd die trying.

But, if instead, a woman chooses to turn away from the fire? If she's sick of the embers scorching her, of the smoke choking her voice—well, then she's chosen darkness. The blackened forest. The crone.

Unnatural. Aberrant, even. She's not a *real* woman.

Bile rises in my throat as I carry on, following the pull, which is now a frayed rope spilling from my guts. I stumble as it yanks me deeper into the dark, toward my future. Toward myself.

The crone is sad. She's isolated. She's lived her entire life alone with nobody to care for—and nobody to care for her.

She's selfish and a burden and everything that's wrong with modern society.

I'm moving quicker now, unable to escape the cruel truth—I am not worthy of being a woman. I'm not willing to die in the fire to fulfill my purpose. And the universe knows it. The spindly trees stand closer together now, snatching at my skin and hair as I whip through them. Still, the bloody rope yanks harder, not caring about the wetness of my cheeks. The branches squeeze around me, stealing my breath, but forward I go until I can't take anymore. I'm suffocating, drowning in my own tears.

And then the dragging stops.

The trees have parted. The rope lies still, one end dangling from my belly, the other held by a wizened woman with wild grey hair that falls past her shoulders. She gives it a tug with her wrinkled hand, reeling me in until I'm mere inches from her. Shaking, I stare at my feet, refusing to meet her eye. Avoiding what I'm sure is an ugly, scarred woman with only pain and suffering and loneliness to thrust upon me.

She drops the rope, lifting her hand to strike me, and I cower.

"Please—no," I croak, falling to my knees. My stomach churns as I bury my face in my hands. "I know I'm empty. Not worthy. Unnatural. But please, don't you think that's enough? You don't need to hurt me more."

Instead of the strike, her hand lays softly on my shoulder, and warmth spreads through me. Her touch isn't harsh or demanding, it's tender and guiding as she urges me to my feet. Confused, I rise, and she cups my cheek with her soft palm.

"Look at me." Her voice is like water trickling over me, washing away my fear.

I will myself to obey and find a proud woman standing before me, stroking my cheek with her thumb. With her raised chin and her shoulders back, she radiates strength and confidence. The lines in her face aren't ugly; they show her courage and wisdom. Her deep brown eyes hold a spark of defiance, as if challenging the world to just try to beat her down. She won't stand for it. She knows her worth.

But there's more, a kindness in her voice and touch. A gentle understanding in her gaze.

"Do you think I'm a selfish coward?" she asks. "Do you think I've been banished to this forest to live alone? That I'm not worthy of a full and happy life?"

My chin trembles as I stare at her, unsure of what to say. There must be some mistake, this can't be the crone who's been calling to me. Everyone told me she's a nasty witch, that she's bitter and hateful. This woman is anything but that. Her mere presence eases my worries and shame.

Like a mother.

I reel away from her, hiding my face. "There's been a mistake. You aren't the crone. I'm not meant for you. I'm barren. I have no child to mother, to guide through this world and nurture into the person they're meant to be."

She tilts her head, but her face holds empathy, not confusion. "There hasn't been a mistake. I'm your crone. I'm every bump and bruise and scar inside you. I'm your empty womb and even emptier heart."

"I should hate you," I reply, not feeling the words. How could I hate someone like her?

"Why?"

When I have no answer, she gives me a kind smile. "It's enough, you know. To just be you." She quirks a brow. "To embrace the person *you* are meant to be."

I want to scoff at her.

But she takes my hand, and a warm breeze whispers over me, ruffling my twig-matted hair. Stars blink to life in the sky above us, and the gnarled trees at the edge of the clearing don't look so scary now. Their skeletal frames hold stark beauty, showing the world that despite the inferno, they're still here. Still standing. Still proud.

And they're not alone, like I'd always assumed. A woodpecker perches on the branch nearest us, bobbing its red head, and two jackrabbits bound between the trunks in a game of tag. Several people come into view. They wander in the long grass, plucking little white flowers and weaving them into each other's hair. Their easy smiles make my heart pinch with longing. When I look closely, what I thought was dead is actually teeming with life.

The world would be missing that beauty without these trees. This community—no, this family. Something only seconds ago I deemed aberrant and terrifying.

The crone squeezes my fingers. "Shall we go for a walk? Let me show you what it's like here, away from the fire. It's a safe place, where you bring your own light to share."

I nod. The rope drops from my stomach, sinking into the grass. We step over it without a thought, and I follow the crone into the twisted forest, which has always been part of me. Not a cold, hateful, lonely existence, but my home waiting for me with crooked—but loving—open arms.

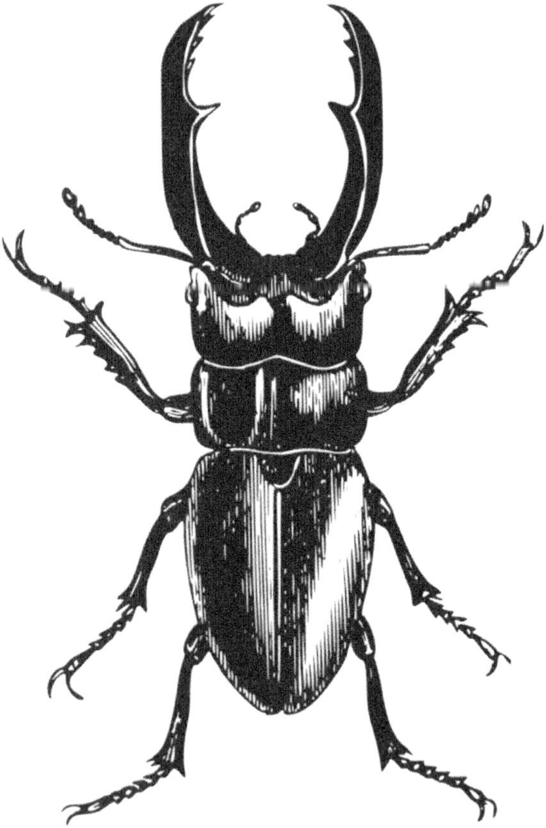

Persephone, Queen of
—I Don't know—
Some Bugs
... Alex Benarzi

Lesson — never go full Persephone.

The river rushes above me, contained by the glass ceiling of my prison kingdom. It's day now: the light skips across the river's surface, errant beams streaking down past the water into our home of moss and sand. Above me, along the shore, there's likely a man walking his dog; a couple hand-in-hand, saying everything in silence; a child getting too close to the edge and retreating in fear.

Smart kid.

I'm sorry if I sound bitter. I don't mean to be. It's just—I didn't think it would be this cold.

I thought it would at least be exciting. Except, I'm not in the Underworld, but under the Elbow River. Except I wasn't given a pomegranate, but a shot of leaves, a dead bug, blood, and (I think) a Werther's Original wrapper, all diluted in river water. Except, there was no scary Hades, brooding Hades, sexy Hades, or any form of misunderstood deity. I got Tim and Tina (I've changed their names to protect their identities). And worst of all, no grieving mother bringing the blight of winter to the world. Not even a pity hailstorm.

Anyone who tells you Persephone was kidnapped is full of poop. There she was, a "young maiden," which, when adjusted for inflation, puts her around thirty. She was "nice" and "smart," which, when translated to English, means she was alone, hated by daddy Zeus and pitied by her myriads of stepsiblings because she was eternally alone. And there she was, the maid of honour for yet another friggin' stepsister, planning a wedding that was supposed to be "rustically elegant," which, when thought of practically, means diddly squat. And there she was, gathering wildflowers somewhere in Bragg Creek, inhaling the intoxicating scene. Twittering birds replaced bickering family. The floral pallet replaced the sickly scent of frosting of too many cake samples. The gentle breeze through shade replaced the merciless sun beating down on them, raising blood pressures as they argued the exact angle at which to place the chuppa. No wonder Persephone volunteered herself to go fetch some useless flowers. And it was no wonder, when a portal opened in the middle of her path, she thought, "I don't know where this leads, but anything is better than here." So, she jumped in, and there was Hades all, "I have seen your suffering, and I am here to help." Or, "Ha ha ha! You foolish girl, I'll teach you to wander off the beaten path." Whatever version you prefer. And finally, after thirty years of being ignored and used by everyone around her, her mother would wake up and realize, "Oh turkey, my daughter is gone. I will let it be known by making the world posterior-cold for nine months of the year. Oh yeah, and when it's not stupid-cold, I will choke the air with smoke and the land with construction barriers. That will teach you to take the most precious girl in the world."

"You're projecting," Tim clicks.

I whirl around to find him lounging on a leaf, his bushy tail his pillow, snacking on a grape twice the size of his mouth.

I bend down to his level, staring into his big, black eyes. "I just thought — I mean — at least Persephone was a queen."

Tim tosses the grape aside and scurries off the leaf. He roots around in the mud, his tiny claws raking away clumps of dirt, until he finds some suitable twigs. Humming the Wedding March, he forms the twigs into a crown, coats it with moss, and decorates it with yellow and red leaves. I lower my head to him. His paws aren't dexterous enough to wrestle the crown onto my head: most of it crumbles away, leaving me with a bird's nest mess on my touched-up blonde.

"It's the thought that counts," Tim flashes a sharp smile, "Your Majesty."

As if to mock his point, sludge rains down on me, washing the broken crown away, and pools at my feet. I sigh and return to my log, staring up at the rush of water.

"Who designed this place anyway?"

Tim jumps up beside me, his tail beating against my lower back. "Who knows. Maybe it was Your Majesty."

"I wouldn't have made it so—gross and wet." I shoo away a persistent mosquito. "And buggy." The mosquito performs a lap around my head and returns to my arm. "Stop it. Your queen commands you to get the fudge away." I flap my arms, but it is too late: just as I drank the blood of the Underriver, so must my blood be taken. "And why is it so small," I shout to the four corners of what is basically an outdoor bachelor apartment.

Tim draws closer and I instinctively scratch his soft fur.

"Fire and brimstone more your aesthetic? A giant lake of lava?" he asks.

"At least we'd be warm."

"You want to go back up."

"No." I search the trees and rocks for some weakness, but my ancient bars stand strong. "I can't."

Tina lands on the far end of the log, and roots through a crevice. She emerges with a worm draped over her beak.

"What's the news from above?" Tim asks.

Tina is the only one of us who can penetrate the barrier.

"Guests have all arrived," Tina says. "They're just waiting on the bride."

I spring to my feet. Instinctively, Tina leaps off the log before realizing that there's no threat. Tim pulls another grape from seemingly nowhere.

Those p'takhs are going ahead with the wedding? "Should we cancel," Mom might have asked after they noticed I was gone. Carrie would have let out her tiny whimper, the dog whistle summoning her father to action. "No, no," he would have said, "we can't get refunds this late in the game. We go ahead: Steph can step in for maid of honour." I grab a fistful of hardpacked dirt and hurl it up at the river. It doesn't make a dent.

Tina lands on my shoulder. "They probably could have used you up there."

I swat at her. "Don't you think I know that?" But she digs her talons into my shoulder. I pick up a rock and try to crack the implacable river, but it does not give way. I scream, summoning an army of dead leaves, which march past us and into the inaccessible distance. I fall to my knees, face-to-face with Tim.

"You could have just stayed above," Tim says, smiling, always smiling.

Why did Persephone jump into the portal? She had a good comfortable life: a stable job in the family business. It wasn't fulfilling. It didn't leave room for advancement. But it was safe. Sure, work and family obligations, such as seemingly never-ending wedding planning, was sucking up all her life so, when she finally had time to herself, she had no more energy than to load whatever the Ancient Greek version of Tik Tok was and watch until she fell asleep—but it was safe, and they were (at least outwardly) proud of her. Who needs anything more?

I pace my lush, barren kingdom. I try to remove Tina's talons from my shirt, or kick Tim from my path, but they cling to me. My loyal subjects.

I snap my fingers. "Comfortable mushroom chair." Nothing happens.

"Doesn't work like that," Tim says. He reaches into the ground and pulls out a strawberry, which he proceeds to bury his face in. Show off.

The sun has shifted. The wedding must have begun by now. I strain to listen but hear only cicadas in the distance. "Let's say," I can feel the words fighting back as I try to force them out. "If I wanted to — could I go back?" Who said that? Some mousy whisper on the wind.

Tina and Tim exchange a look. Tim beckons me to follow and scurries away, heading downriver until he reaches the rocks that bar our path. He jerks his head toward one of the rocks.

"I don't see anything," I say.

"Look down."

I crouch to find a gap between the ground and rock. If I flatten myself and wriggle in, assuming the space remains consistent, I might be able to make it through.

"So that's it. I crawl back on my hands and knees?"

"No," Tim says, and for the first time since I met him (about a day ago), his smile drops. "You must worm your way back in."

"I can't."

"I know."

I return to my log and look up at the river rushing by, wishing I had jumped in the river instead of the muddy hole.

I clench my teeth, dig my hands into the dirt, and pull out an apple. I rub it against my muddy, damp sweater. I close my eyes, take a bite. Texture aside, it's sweet. I finish it and pull out another.

Better than wedding cake.

The Moon & the Stars
... Joseph Halden & Rhonda Parrish

The moss was cool and soft as velvet under my multitudinous feet as I undulated across the forest floor. The sighing of the wind was a gentle shushing sound, as though the world was trying to offer me comfort, to ease the weight of my burden. It was not enough, though, not enough to ease the slow, continuous seeping of my heart.

I wished I could look up, to see the stars I knew winked down at me, but lifting my head was an impossibility—all my will and energy being funneled into moving forward through the night. But the moon, the stars I could not see, they illuminated the snail trails and the path enough I could see the detailed crags and crevices of a half-rotten tree, its spongy innards spilled out, half-blocking my way.

Still I kept my feet moving, pausing only when an iridescent beetle scuttled by. I wondered at her speed, her dexterity. The way her green-black shell shone as she moved. Had I ever moved like that, or had I always carried this heaviness in my limbs? I could not remember. The time before my loss was a fog, a nearly opaque curtain that I could not penetrate with my mourning eyes, could not part with feet or memory.

Like the tree, I half-blocked the beetle's path, but like me she would not be deterred. She climbed over top of me, disturbing the fungi which grow upon the collection I carry on my back so that they shook free some of their spores which drifted and danced in the moonlight as she continued on her way leaving behind a soft, spicy scent trail.

I followed the traces deeper into the woods. This night, I had emerged from my grief, from my burrow, to forage. To add to the baubles and shinies I carried which made me feel safe and important for no other in the forest had such treasures, none but me.

The trails led down into a gully, and I wormed down until the walls surrounded me, until it felt as though the tree roots had entwined with the mycelium on my back, hitching a ride because how could the weight of the world matter to someone already carrying so much.

A tiny stream trickled down the gully's belly and where it bent, I found the snails.

Swaying with muted breaths to a suppressed cadence only they could hear, several of them encircled something on the shore. Rippling closer, I made out the body of a snail without a shell, its innards exposed to the cruel cutting air, the wind that suggested gentleness of a world anything but.

Although their friend had not yet passed, the snails were mourning the inevitable.

My tears thickened the gully's stream until the water brushed the side of the wheezing snail—they could do nothing, and I ached seeing such a rippling mirror of my experiences.

A few of the snails turned slowly toward me, taking a few moments to scan the breadth of all I carried. My bodily awareness wandered in traces following the path of their gaze, and I remembered one of the many shells nested in my soil.

So little to be done. But there *was* something.

I twisted my shoulder and, with an inner groan echoing tectonic movements, I reached back and felt for the shell. Pinch. Pull. Wince. I squeezed my eyes shut to drown out the pain as I tore it free.

A sharp stab, then tingling. I brought the shell in front of me and saw in its reflection stars that I'd known were still there, but knowing and seeing and feeling are very different things.

No time to waste on this new sensation, though, or this burst of energy might leave as a dispersing spore cloud.

Bending down further was easy. I'd had lots of practice.

I moistened the shell in the stream and while most of the shell-less snail's friends shrank away, a brave few straightened up close to him. Worry not, little ones, I am not the crushing boulder I may appear to be.

The suffering snail's friends moved slowly, tentatively aside, their antennae tasting the air, measuring my intentions, and I reached out slowly, slowly, holding the new shell before me. The trumpet-shaped shell, opalescent inside and violet out, looked too large for the suffering mollusk, but I inhaled a deep breath of petrichor, steadied my grip and slid the shell on the snail. The little mollusk disappeared deep inside, but I felt its relieved hum through the shelf, a thrill of excitement at being protected and held. Of being home. Of having a chance, however small. It was a chance smaller than the tree root hairs peeking out of the gully walls, but it was still a chance.

I set the newly shelled snail down at the edge of the stream and stepped back, mindful of where I placed every one of my feet lest I cause more damage than I had cured. The mollusk was immediately surrounded by friends who tapped and touched the new, different shell gently, lovingly.

Not wanting to interfere, I continued upstream, marveling at how much lighter I felt—far more than the weight of one shell. How much less my perpetual heartache. Distracted as I was, probing the edges of my pain, I nearly missed it when the wind carried the sound of soft sobbing to me. I knew that flavour of pain, and I turned toward it, the pang in my chest shifting from one of pure sorrow to a desire to help, to ease *another's* sorrows.

Beneath the forest's canopy, deep in the shadows where only the faintest echoes of star and moonlight penetrate, I found the toad.

It lay on its side, bulbous eyes opening briefly before bursting into another sob at the scene before it. What had clearly been a fallen log was torn to pieces and claw marks scarred every scrap strewn about the area. The ground had been torn up, all the low-level shrubs uprooted and stacked in a pile where the gully's water pooled.

This had been the toad's home, once. A secluded wet patch of dense shrubbery beneath a fallen log, with countless nooks and crannies to hide and store and sleep.

Familiar, common destruction. Still devastating.

I sat down beside the toad, craning forward to keep holding all I carried. I'm sorry, warty one. I understand your loss but feel as powerless as you. The only thing I know to ease your suffering is to sit beside you with it, for a while.

So I sat, and the toad cried beside me.

How long had you lived here, toad? Long enough for the loss to cut out a part of you.

Had you lived here with others? If you tell me, maybe I can do more. But though we share this earth, we might as well be mountains apart for all that we can really know each other's innermost suffering. Glimpses maybe, but never fully knowing.

Something nudged my side.

A snail, familiar—had it followed me from the stream?—pointing with its eyestalks up at all I carried. Nearby, several snails craned their necks up and down as though reaching for something too high. Puzzled, I leaned sideways toward them to see if there was something I couldn't yet glean. They quickened, excited and encouraged. I leaned more until the weight of all I carried graced the ground for the first time in many moons.

The snails nodded and moved up onto my hoard, high and around where I couldn't see. I gasped. They should not be there.

A dozen pine-needles pricked my treasures, and then plucked. Before I knew what was happening, a line of snails moved off my baggage, each carrying something small, from shells to plants to flat rocks to fungi.

When they nudged the mourning toad, I knew what was happening.

I felt each removal as a sharp pain followed by a dull, throbbing and I wished it to stop—how much more could I bear? How much more could I carry? But, just as I was shifting to stand, intending to shake the snails off, to take back what was mine, a little snail in an over-sized trumpet-shaped shell slid toward the toad. The snail was holding one of my very special agates—shiny and red—toward her.

Seeing it, the toad's sobbing slowed.

When the little snail stacked the stone on top of a slab of empty honeycomb another snail had retrieved from my back a moment before, the toad sat upright. She watched the snails, eyes wide and blinking, and I stayed my movement. Watched as the snails took the things I had gathered in my sorrow and planted them like seeds to grow a home for the toad.

It could never fully replace what had been lost, but it was something. And from where I lay on the ground, while the snails slithered over me and relieved me of some of my armor, through a tiny opening in the forest canopy, I could see the moon. And the stars.

Extinction Burst
... Robert Fields Byrne

I stopped trimming the thick grass around the house. My mom would say that spiders live there, and regular hedging keeps them away. Their furtive darting startled my young self. I never understood where they were going or what they were doing or why. So I came of tool-wielding age, and I was shown how to trim. She was right, of course. As parents often are, in a funny way. More than last summer nested in the taller grasses that grew around the outside of the house. But they stopped showing inside. And there were fewer ants pilfering the cereal and fewer mosquito bites in mornings after windows stayed open.

The garden grew thin early in the summer. She never got soft fruits or herbs to grow right—said she was unused to the soil around here. Too much clay. So it was mostly flowers and soon they were all picked for her anyway. It just looked like shadows in the scans. I still think the doctor was lying, and it was all in her head. It just looked like shadows until it wasn't, and even then maybe it was. Maybe she grew weary of the maintenance of life. And so I grew weary of maintaining the garden she left.

Late in season the humidity attracts thunderstorms, and they walk together through the prairies and shake everything loose. This marriage proved a catalyst to the condition I found the hummingbird in. That morning, I finally noticed the feeder covered in dark mold from long unchanged sugar water and the small body beneath. A once slender emerald frame bloated into mushes and slimes, still held together with skin and soft feathers, lying on wide dandelion leaves in the unmowed lawn. I had also been meaning to pull the weeds. Though only where they showed to neighbors walking by or visiting family. But as the hummingbird lay with wings outstretched on thick arms of the weeds that grew, I was sure it would have fully decomposed without the overgrowth's embrace.

In both hands I carried the hummingbird to the prairie at the end of the street, where I hope it still now lies, tucked in the base of the oak tree at the beginning of the trail. It was likely eaten by a coyote and maybe my mold made the poor coyote sick, too. I had come this far already, though only to bury a thing long since passed, so I started down the prairie path I had not walked in many months. Absently wandering for the second casualty. As the sun warmed me for the first time in many months, my gait reopened. The thought occurred that perhaps I had simply gone to soothe the sour regret of neglect, and that it made no difference at all to the carcass whether it lay in the yard, or tucked in the base of an oak tree, or anywhere.

Over a crest in the trail, at this particular time late in the afternoon, the sun glares between trees at my back and throws a sepia camouflage on the prairie grasses sloping below. I came over the crest and into the camouflage and saw her closely observing a tall goldenrod bordering the trail. She leaned forward on tip toes to peer intently at the stalk. Despite loose hiking attire, the neat posture was immediately recognizable. I had always envied the way she carried herself. As though she is always as tall as she is.

"If this isn't the funniest little thing. We were wondering where you'd been, worried we wouldn't get to see you until next semester. Do you live around here?"

"Something like that. I'm just down the street from where the path starts."

"By yourself? I thought I was missing you all summer because you were back with your parents."

"Oh, yeah." I sighed deeply. She squinted and cocked her head. "Well, my mom passed, and dad moved in with whoever he had already been dating. You know how dads are. So it's just left to me. The house, I suppose."

"Sweet girl, I'm so sorry." She grabbed my hand, and we matched funeral smiles. I realized I had been slouching. "I didn't know."

"I didn't tell anyone from our program. It's my fault. It's like there are these things I know I should be doing, but I can't figure out why I should be doing them or which ones I should be doing or not doing. So I haven't really been…" The goldenrod rose where the kept trail grass gave way to wild prairie. I realized I'd been staring unsociably at that transition instead of more actively participating. Cargo pockets draping her short frame plinked and squeaked of slightly rubbing glass. "Sorry. So, what are you doing all the way out here anyway?"

She beamed and her stance widened pridefully. "I'm collecting mosquito samples across different preserves in the county. In their whole lifespan, a mosquito can only travel a half mile from where they are born. If a mosquito tests positive for wolf's blood, we can chart that a wolf was recently within a half mile from where the mosquito was collected. It's my summer project."

"Huh, I would have never thought of that."

"I know! It always bugged me that mosquitos never appeared to serve any functional purpose in the overall ecosystem dynamic. I mean, maybe they do, or always did. We're only students—we have a lot left to learn. But the thought always irked me, right? So, when the county contacted our department for low budget ways of tracking local population movement, I found this method in some old research paper. All these tools and techniques we use to eliminate the little vampires because they annoy and bite us, and these guys figured a way to use this specific function of feeding on blood to gauge the population health of animals that we like more. I mean, how neat, right?"

"No kidding. I really do miss the way you think."

"Then you should have me over sometime. If you're not too busy staring at the ground. How's the house, by the way? How are you keeping up?"

"Most days the house seems fine. If I could figure out what to do with the garden. I've just been letting it go. It's all weeds and bugs and dying things and no more flowers. I'm worried the neighbors will find it unsightly. You took the classes—what should I spray the intruders with?"

"These intruders being the native species lying long dormant under pesticides? Fuck your neighbors. People are funny. They just want to see trimmed lawns and sweet smells and forget what that entails. Most flowers give fewer nutrients back to the ground than they take. The soil gets hard to work with that way, after a while. Besides, things die and are eaten and fertilize the soil and other real things can grow. We drive away all the small things in the world, but where do they go?"

"I never really considered it. Apparently back to my yard, once I started letting it grow."

"Like who knows what would happen if we genetically bred all the mosquitoes sterile. At the least I wouldn't get to do my little project out here." She squeezed my hand. "I'd love to come see your new garden. I really do have to get to a few more spots today. Call me, yeah?"

Dusk was fading by the time I got back to the house. Myriad shadows splayed in all directions, but the lone porchlight watched over me as I wiped the slime mold and replaced the sugar water. Crouching under the feeder, I lifted the large dandelion plant by the base to pull full taproot and revealed several small brown cap mushrooms under the folded leaves. They were soft and new and perfectly formed and directly under where the carcass was leaking decompositional fluids. A small wolf spider inched out from under one of the caps. It must have been feeding on the previously swarming flies. I paused, observing for a moment unexpectedly slow and careful movement as it crept back under the spore. I released the dandelion back to where it was and switched off the porchlight on the way inside. In the morning, I thought I saw a small hummingbird flit to and from the feeder, but it may have been another shadow. I changed the sugar water every day anyway. And for the rest of the season the yard stayed lit through the nights with constellations of lightning bugs.

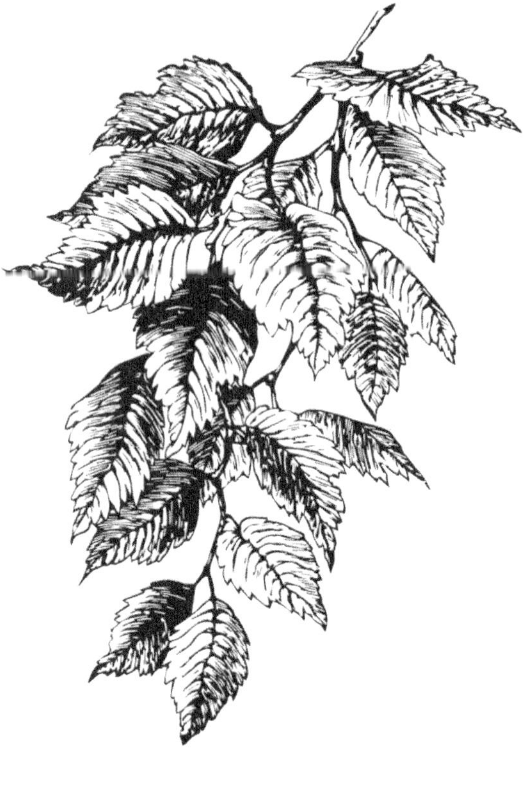

Forest Magic
... Valerie Hunter

Violet had been living in the forest cottage for two years when she received the letter from her older brother John. She went into the village once a fortnight to meet with clients—she made good money as a seamstress—and the letter was waiting for her at the general store.

She didn't open it until she got home, and John's words seemed to fill the cottage like a poisonous miasma. He'd decided that his oldest son, Lester, should come to stay with her. Violet must be lonely, in need of a male protector.

What he didn't say, but which Violet understood just as clearly, was that Lester was ready for a wife and a home of his own. Perhaps he was betrothed already, or perhaps he intended to find a girl in the village, but either way, he wanted Violet's home. She would stay as a housekeeper and later as a nursemaid to the children, just as she had done for John and his wife all those years, but the cottage would not be her own anymore, because her brother believed it should never have been hers to begin with.

When Violet had inherited the cottage from an aunt she hardly remembered, John had advised her to sell the property or rent it out. When she'd decided to live there instead, he insisted that it was unladylike, that she had an obligation to his family, that she'd never survive on her own.

She'd gone anyway. The cottage was small and smothered in ivy, but it was soundly built and the perfect home for someone who had never had a space of her own before. When she wasn't sewing, she was outside tending her vegetable garden or gathering mushrooms and berries. She learned to harvest honey without getting stung, to dye fabric with madder root and walnut hulls, to appreciate the strange noises of the insects and wildlife that surrounded her. She wasn't lonely, and she didn't need anyone's protection.

Violet wasn't sure how to make John see that. She spent the evening working on the quilt she was making for herself, not orderly patchwork but a conglomeration of scraps fitted together piecemeal and embroidered with her finest threads. She spent hours creating a collection of tiny fungi on a triangle of brown velvet, and by the time she went to bed, she had the inkling of an idea.

The next morning, she walked deeper into the forest, towards the other cottage. Another woman lived there, around the same age as Violet; they'd never spoken, but Violet had seen her several times when she went berrying, and she'd seen others there, too, including several men.

Today the cottage was quiet. Violet hesitated; she should have introduced herself long ago, been neighborly before she wanted anything from this woman. But the woman had never come to see her, either.

She knocked. The woman answered, beckoning her inside. The walls were lined with dolls, some as small as acorns, some with wings like moths, others realistic and life-sized, all of them marvels. A worktable was crowded with tools and implements.

The woman's name was Elowyn, but she said Violet should call her Wyn. Violet explained her predicament, her sudden need for a man. "I thought you might know…"

"My companions aren't real," Wyn said, motioning towards the dolls. "Just wood and cloth and some clockwork mechanisms. But perhaps that's all you need."

Violet had been hoping for flesh and blood, but clockwork was better than nothing. On the appointed morning, Wyn brought over a broad-shouldered man with piercing eyes. When she wound a key in his back, he went about chopping a fallen tree into kindling, every movement sure and smooth.

"Surely that's not just clockwork!" Violet said, staring.

Wyn shrugged. "Clockwork and a bit of forest magic."

Wyn left, and Lester arrived shortly thereafter, looking smug. He had always looked that way, even as a baby when Violet changed his nappies.

"I'm afraid your journey was in vain," she said sweetly. "I have no need of you, because I've found myself a husband." She motioned to the strapping clockwork man, who continued to chop wood with gusto.

Lester gaped and spluttered as though it was unbelievable that Aunty Violet could ever marry. Violet took advantage of his befuddlement to turn him gently around, telling him he could catch the next train if he hurried. He left.

She returned the woodcutter to Wyn, thanking her profusely, but her triumph was short-lived. The following week there was another letter. John chided her for marrying without telling him, insisted that he must meet this man, deem him suitable.

When Violet went back to Wyn for help, Wyn frowned. "My creations don't speak. They couldn't fool anyone under close scrutiny."

"Not even with forest magic?" Violet asked, desperation dripping from each word.

Wyn sat back, considering. "Make him a fine shirt," she said finally, "and I'll see what I can do."

Violet went home, glad for a task to keep her busy. She looked through all her fabric, but she didn't have enough of anything suitable.

Her gaze kept returning to her patchwork. It was nearly large enough to cover her bed, but she hadn't quilted it yet. She could cut a shirt from it.

She did it before she could reconsider, crafting the shirt to the measurements Wyn had provided, then embroidering squirrels and snails and beetles and briars wherever it looked too bare. She carved buttons from beech wood, painting a stag on each one.

When she finished, she feared it looked like a fool's livery, but it was too late to make something else. She knocked at Wyn's door, but there was no answer, so she left the shirt there, trying not to worry that Wyn had given up on her—trying not to wonder if this would be the last night she'd spend alone in her own home.

The next morning, she answered the knock at her door to find the woodcutter wearing the shirt she'd made him. It no longer looked foolish. He no longer looked like an automaton. He'd looked lifelike before, but now he looked fully human.

He touched his lips to her hand. "My lady." His voice contained the multitudes of the forest—the susurration of the leaves, the song of the toads, the trill of the insects.

"What should I call you?" she asked.

"Husband," he said simply.

She laughed. "You need a name."

"Whatever you choose."

"Sylvanus," she decided. His hand was fleshy and warm, but she thought she could feel the wood at its core, the branches of his skeleton.

He smiled at her, a radiant smile, and she smiled back, trying not to worry that he might dissolve before her eyes.

John arrived, and Violet let herself fade into the background where he thought she belonged. She served tea and scones, let Sylvanus do the talking. John listened to him, and gradually Violet saw something change in her brother's expression. He was convincing himself that the cottage was too inconsequential for Lester, and that he was glad to be able to hand the responsibility of Violet over to this man.

She wanted to shout, remind him of her existence, how she'd kept his house and minded his children all those years, how she was worthy of this home regardless of whether she was married. She wanted to pour scalding tea in his lap and order him to go away. But she held her tongue and smiled demurely because that was what it took to win.

When John left, he clapped Sylvanus on the back and didn't thank Violet for the tea. She knew he would never return because she didn't belong to him anymore, was no longer useful to him. Hallelujah.

After letting out a long breath, Violet walked Sylvanus back to Wyn's. He was silent, clinging to her hand like he'd be lost without her.

She knocked on Wyn's door, but there was still no answer. Should she leave him here, like she'd done with the shirt? She stood on tiptoes and kissed his cheek. "Thank you."

He unbuttoned the shirt. It slipped off like a skin, and Violet stared, transfixed, as Sylvanus changed before her eyes.

Not an automaton.

Not a man.

Wyn.

"Clockwork can only do so much," Wyn said, pressing the shirt into Violet's hands. "But you put forest magic of your own into this."

Violet's head swam; words seemed to have left her. So she kissed Wyn instead, on the lips this time, and felt the magic flow between them.

When they pulled apart, Wyn said, "I hope you'll visit again under more pleasing circumstances, my lady."

Violet nodded, then passed her back the shirt. "This belongs to you."

Wyn smiled. It was Sylvanus's smile, though nothing else about them was similar.

The sun was setting, and the forest was dappled with shadows, but Violet basked in the light of that smile; the glow of their shared magic.

A Mountain's Plea
... A.J. McCutchen

The witch's hut blended seamlessly into the woods, as if Nature herself had woven it into the fabric of the forest. Twisted tree branches, gnarled with age, formed the skeletal structure, while mud, clay, and moss filled the gaps, creating a living, breathing entity. Weeds and vines snaked up the walls, as if trying to reclaim the hut for the earth. The roof was a tangle of leaves, branches, and feathers, camouflaging the hut from above and by some means providing protection from rain to the interior of the abode. In the center of this organic maze, a crooked chimney reached high into the canopy above. If the cloistered nature of the hut and the natural camouflage weren't enough to keep the place hidden from unlikely passersby, the witch's subtle magics and hexes would take care of the rest.

   The two forest spirits waited outside the hut, their nebulous forms fluttering on the wind. There was no discernable entrance into the witch's home. No clear door on which the spirits could knock. The living house seemed to react to the presence of the spirits. Its leaves and vines reached almost imperceptibly toward them.

"Are you sure this is a good idea?" Piru asked, her voice like a gentle rain.

"No," Vila admitted, "but what choice do we have?"

"Who's out there?" came a voice from inside the contorted hut.

Before the spirits could answer, a crow cawed somewhere in the distance. Another repeated the sound, this time slightly closer. Then another, closer still. And finally, a black bird somewhere in the branches overhead joined in, and the air around the hut started to buzz as the hut altered itself. Roots shifted, branches bent, vines retracted, all in unison to create the rough shape of a doorway. Inside, the spirits could see only darkness, interrupted periodically by the yellow-orange light of a flickering flame somewhere inside. The hill witch emerged. Her tattered gray ankle-length dress could have been hiding any number of things within its billowed folds and myriad pockets, all adding volume to her short and thin frame underneath. All this was covered by an apron which was stained with so many different colors that its original hue was now a secret. Her hair was a matted mess with twigs and feathers woven throughout.

The witch regarded the two spirits for a moment. "Did I summon you?" she asked finally, wiping her hands on the apron as she spoke. It was an honest question. She really didn't seem to know.

"You did not," Vila admitted. "We have come to ask for your help."

The hill witch's gaze narrowed. "What kind of help?" she asked carefully.

Piru came forward, her ethereal form undulating in the breeze. "To the east, a mountain is dying," she said, her voice a gentle lament. "The forest there has been razed."

The witch's expression turned skeptical. "What business is it of mine? And what could I do that two forest spirits could not?"

Vila's form fluttered with urgency. "The wounds in the mountain run deep. Too deep for us. Our domain is above."

"And the wounds are infected with the malice of your kind," Piru added. "The soil is bad. The water under the mountain is spoiled."

"My kind?" the witch answered resentfully. "Witches destroyed your forest?"

"Not witches. Machines and their humans," Vila said.

"I see," the witch said slowly, more to herself than to her visitors. As she gazed through the trees at something unseen, a harvestman crawled from her hairline and down her neck onto her shoulder and began bobbing up and down. The witch paid no attention. "I will help," she said finally. "But I should pack first."

The witch hurried back into her hut and after a few moments of searching she reemerged with a cloth sack tied shut with a thin rope. She looked around the grounds for a moment until she found what seemed to be a random stone half buried in the damp ground. She knelt down and lifted the stone, prompting a small number of pill bugs and one particularly annoyed centipede to scurry away. The witch opened the bag and placed it on the ground near where the stone had been. She scooped a handful of soil from the ground and began to rub the earth between her leathery hands, while muttering something under her breath. The small patch of dirt where the stone had once been started to heave. Suddenly it erupted like an egg sac and thousands upon thousands of creatures of the earth began pouring out. Beetles, worms, centipedes, grubs, ants of all kinds issued forth from the opening, and they all marched directly into the witch's bag. As they filed in, the bag lurched and bucked, but it never showed any sign of becoming full. Indeed, after several minutes of swallowing an impossible number of crawling things, the bag looked no different than when the witch brought it from her hut.

When the last bug had crawled in, the witch picked up the bag (which should have been an impossible task). She held it to her ear, and she shook it. Displeased, she furrowed her brow and began looking around the grounds once again. She walked here and there, hunched over and looking intently at the ground until she found the perfect spot. She clawed at the ground with long thin fingers, digging a hole as quick as any clawed animal. Her hand darted into the hole, and she produced a single cricket, which she held gingerly between her finger and thumb. She regarded the cricket for a moment before tossing it into the bag with the others.

The hill witch walked sprightly to the spirits and, with a grin, said, "I'm ready. Lead the way."

Roadkill Rising
... Brent Nichols

The head comes off when I tug on it. That's how I know it's ready.

The bones have been in the ditch for a while. The flesh is gone, and spring grass has grown up through the jaw and the eye sockets. I brace myself and jerk upward, tearing grass away as I stand in triumph. I'm pleased to see that the jawbone is still attached on one side.

Tires crunch on gravel behind me, and I turn, wincing. There's nobody I *want* to meet during this particular chore, but the truck I see takes the warmth out of the morning sunshine. It stops behind my own truck and the passenger window rolls down. I paste on a bland, unconcerned expression and pretend I'm not just about on fire with embarrassment.

The driver is a local knuckle-dragger named Jeff. I ignore him while he sneers at me. My sister sits beside him, eyebrows lifted in precise arcs meant to show a blend of concern and dismay. She says, "Everything alright?"

I look down at the moose skull in my hands. What does she think, I've been attacked by a skeleton? "I'm fine."

Jeff shakes his head. I go on ignoring him.

The look on Jennifer's face is a bit harder to dismiss. "What are you doing?" she says gently.

I've tried explaining my art to her. There's no point in repeating myself. I stare at her instead and wait for this to be over.

"I worry about you." She shoots a quick glance at Jeff. "We all do."

The earnest pity in her eyes grates on me. I shift my gaze to a rusty spot on her door.

"Britney gets back tomorrow. What's she going to think when she sees …." She gestures with a stiff arm, taking in the skull, the scattered bones behind me, and all of me from head to foot. "This?"

I have no idea how my teenage daughter will react to my latest creations, or to my ongoing work. I shrug.

"She'll be appalled," says Jennifer. "And embarrassed."

"He's sick." Jeff, apparently feeling left out, leans past his wife and glares at me. "He's a freak. He needs to be locked up."

Jennifer looks from Jeff to me and back to Jeff. By the look on her face there's more she wants to say, but there's only one way to shut Jeff up.

She closes her window.

Jeff hits the gas and the truck takes off, showering me with a derisive spray of gravel.

I've got a dirt pad behind the shop where I let my raw materials ripen. The birds know where it is, and there's easy access for the ants. I put the moose bones with the rest.

"Morning, boys," I say as I round the corner of the shop. The barbershop quartet is a work in progress, four human-like figures put together mostly with deer bones. I want all four heads to be different. So far, I've scrounged up a deer's skull with stubby two-pronged antlers, a cow skull with curving horns, and an elk.

"Don't worry, Harry." I've started calling the fourth man Headless Harry. I pat his shoulder as I go by. "I found a head for you. It just needs a couple weeks with the ants, and we'll finish you up."

Harry doesn't reply. I go into the front yard, where I spend a moment gazing up at my prize display. One more day until Britney arrives. She'll be here for the summer. I try to see the yard as she will see it.

She'll be appalled. And embarrassed.

There's still time to scrap everything. Haul it all to the dump. Or hide it in a corner of the shop and try to introduce Britney to the idea gently. Maybe not spring it on her all at once.

I look up at my finest piece and think about snipping the wires I tied with such meticulous care. I imagine shoving it all in a dark corner and acting like I'm ashamed. My hands tighten into fists, and I shake my head.

I've barely seen my daughter in two years. She and her mother live in the city, while I, not unlike the moose, have lain in a devastated sprawl, broken, my pieces scattered. But my barbershop quartet has shown me that the shattered can rise again. They can even be beautiful.

"It will be fine," I tell myself. I pretend I'm certain. "It will be great."

🍄

Jessica's car rolls to a stop at the end of the driveway. The doors remain closed as I trudge down the outstretched finger of gravel. I feel as hollowed-out and empty as the moose.

When I'm a dozen steps from the car the doors swing open. My ex-wife is busy avoiding my eyes. I ignore her. My daughter fills my vision.

She has her back to me as she tugs suitcases from the back seat. She's tall—tall enough that it startles me, though her limbs don't have much more flesh than my barbershop quartet. She's familiar and strange all at once, and I stop and gawk at her like I've never seen a kid before.

Then all the luggage is unloaded, and we're out of distractions. For a long awkward moment, I stare at Britney and both of them stare at me. Jessica never does speak. She just gets back into the car.

I barely notice when she drives away.

Speaking to my daughter shouldn't scare me. I think of my moose, her tongue long gone, and feel a wry kinship. Then I grab a suitcase and a duffel bag, and we start the long walk to the house.

The barbershop quartet is hidden by the bulk of the shop. In a moment, however, we'll get past the aspen in the yard, and she'll see my masterpiece.

She'll be appalled. And embarrassed.

I glance at Britney. She's looking at me, her lips moving like she's having as much trouble as me figuring out what to say.

Then her gaze slides sideways. Her eyes widen, her feet stop moving, and her jaw hangs slack.

I stop as well, and we look at the roof of the shop.

An astronaut stands on the crest of the roof, silver coveralls gleaming in the sun, a helmet under one arm. Hooves protrude from the sleeves of the coveralls. The head is the skull of a whitetail buck, the bone dazzling as the sunshine hits it.

A magnificent rack of antlers spreads above him. It makes the helmet a bit silly, but that's not the point.

I'm proud of my creation. I can't help it. I even manage a grin, before I look nervously at my daughter.

Her forehead scrunches up. She glances at me, then returns her attention to the astronaut. She speaks at last, her voice tinged with disbelief. "Did you … make that?"

I nod, knowing she'll see it in the corner of her eye. "I call him Buck Rogers."

She turns to look at me. Her eyes are very wide. I hold my breath.

"Oh my god, Dad!" Her face lights up. "That's awesome!"

The Eerie Wood
... Emily A. Grigsby

She saw it again, just out of the corner of her eye. The third time this week. She couldn't make out shape, color, or any sort of defining characteristics; but she knew she saw something. She folded up Papa's damp shirt in her arms and stared at the forest. Her brothers call it "the Eerie Wood," their parents don't let them enter in. Though Lessie didn't view it so much as eerie, but more enchanting and bewitching in a magnificent kind of way. She watched it for what felt like ages for any sign of the blur, the only movement was the leaves and brushes in the breeze.

"Lessie!" The shout from her brother made her body and heart jump, "Aren't you done yet? Mama's calling everyone for breakfast."

She hurriedly finished hanging the wash, gathered the basket and extra pins, and started toward the house. Turning to gaze at the wood again for just a minute more. *I wonder what's just beyond that dark shadow of the first row of trees?*

A question she'd pondered hundreds of times, but with a growl of her stomach she again set off for the house.

The day passed slowly. Being the oldest, and a proper young lady, she had many responsibilities. Washing, cooking, cleaning, planting. She didn't mind it very much, except with Mama being busy with the baby and her brothers working with Papa, she was often lonely. She had been born at this house just over fourteen years ago. It was a pleasant house, always busy and loud with five young boys and a colicky baby brother. Their only neighbor, Miss Thorne, lived in a small, ivy ridden cottage at the bottom of the small slope towards the wood. She mostly kept to herself, occasionally coming out to pull the overgrown ivy off her door and windows. Lessie was always intrigued with Miss Thorne. She would watch her from afar, watch as she hobbled out her front door, her long grey hair past her waist.

Finally, evening approached, Lessie slowly took down the wash from the line, examining the wood. No signs of movement tonight. Did she imagine the vague blur she saw this morning? She so wanted to find out. She looked toward the house; the boys were still working with Papa way in the fields and Mama had barely started dinner when Lessie came out to check on the clothesline. *Mama doesn't want us to go into the woods, but getting a little closer to get a better look will be alright.* She justified to herself. She took a few steps, then a few more but faster this time. Before she knew it, she was sprinting toward the wood like she was being pulled in by an invisible fishing line. She was so close she could feel the cool, heavy, wet air misting from the forest. She could see some fog over what looked like a bog of some sort. She was running trance-like when…

"Lessie! Darlin'!" Miss Thorne gave Lessie a big grin. Lessie stopped so suddenly she almost fell backwards. She was out of breath more from the scare than the running. "Where you runnin' off to this time of night? The Forest sure is beautiful during twilight, but I wouldn't if I was you." Her teeth large, crooked and yellowing. Her smile-lines and forehead wrinkles long and deep. The streams of the setting sun made her silver-gray hair almost glow. Lessie noticed something else glowing, a necklace around Miss Thorne's neck. On it a flat, round pendant of some kind.

"Miss Thorne! I…I…I was…" *What was I doing?* Lessie wondered to herself midsentence. She realized she wasn't thinking clearly. This should have alarmed her, but it excited her. Miss Thorne gave out a hearty laugh, a cross between a chuckle and a cackle. It made Lessie smile and almost laugh herself, if she hadn't still been out of breath.

"I know what you was doin', child. I know what you was longin' fer. The Forest has a way about her…" Her statement trailed off as she turned to marvel at the wood. She looked for a few moments then shook her head violently. "No, no, I too old fer that now." She studied Lessie's face. "I was jus' 'bout yer age when I felt her callin' me, too. Ha! Was I ever that young?" She started shuffling towards her cottage relying heavily on her cane. "Young back, strong legs…Oh hullo there Hopscotch! Fern! Have a peaceful night." Lessie looked down as two large toads hopped away into the woods. Miss Thorne stopped. She turned her head just enough for Lessie to see the silhouette of her face in the fading light. "Listen to me girl—the Wood is not fer the faint a heart. Yer mother is right for not wantin' you ta venture therein." She paused, "However, if you must…start yer course at daylight…" She opened her mouth as if to say on but just continued onto her home.

Lessie didn't know what to think laying in bed that night. She could hardly sleep; when she did close her eyes, she would see Miss Thorne laughing or toads disappearing into the forest. At first light Lessie slipped out of bed, careful to not make a sound. She pulled on her shoes and overcoat. It was a chilly and foggy morning. The slope leading down to the forest was slick with morning dew, she came to the beautiful hazy wood quickly. She looked around—she didn't see Miss Thorne and her cottage was still dark. *I will go see what's beyond the trees and be back before breakfast.* Then, with confidence mixed with fear, she stepped into the Eerie Wood.

Her daydreams could never compare with this. The lavish greens, the rich browns. Bright green moss dotted with small round red and white mushrooms. She took several more steps into this paradise, then several more. She happened upon a stream. Algae-covered rocks made it difficult to pass; dragonflies zoomed, cattails stood tall and motionless, toads speedily hopped away. *I wonder if they know Hopscotch and Fern?* She hardly noticed the trees becoming so thick it made the sunlight almost non-existent. She ducked under hanging branches, stepped over rotting logs, admired the bats zig-zagging just overhead, and laughed as water fell from the tree's top leaves. She could hardly believe it!

Something glistened in a small ray of sunlight. The much-less-cautious Lessie reached out and moved some sod away from a hollow section of tree trunk. She couldn't make it out, they looked small and round and polished. Before she could investigate further, something hit her on the side of her arm. "Ow!" She pulled her hand away from the treasure.

"Ehhhh!" The creature picked up another rock. "Git away from there, you!" His thin arm barely clearing his long, pointy ear as he threw that one, too. He missed. "Humans ain't welcome here—git back to wherever it is you belong!"

Lessie cocked her head to one side, she had heard tales of fairies, elves, goblins and other such magical beings. This goblin was bigger than what she imagined, probably half her height. "I'm sorry," Lessie stepped away from the tree.

"Hmmph!" Snorted the goblin as he dropped his third rock, turned sharply and started stomping away.

"Wait!" cried Lessie running after him, grabbing her coat tighter around herself. The goblin did not stop—if anything he stomped along more briskly. His skin was dark, green maybe, draped over him was a loose-fitting brown shirt and trousers. She started to lose sight of him—she squinted as she ran faster. Suddenly he was right in front of her, standing on a newly fallen tree.

"What?!" His large dark yellow eyes were almost level with Lessie's light blue ones.

"I…well, I've never been here before, and I'd like to learn more about these woods and, well…you." She smiled. "The forest has been calling to me for years. Miss Thorne said the same thing happened to her when she was young—"

The goblin cut her off, "Adelaide? Adelaide Thorne?" Now *he* was smiling, his long, slender teeth all in a neat row. After a second, he looked at Lessie again, his wide eyes now narrowed, smile gone, "Well, if Adelaide talked to you…then…well…if you can keep up." He spun round and continued on.

Lessie did keep up, barely. She didn't care her shoes were covered in mud, her coat got a rip, and her auburn hair was dirty and wild. The goblin ducked into an opening at the bottom of a massive moss-covered tree trunk. Lessie ducked down, then ducked some more and with a little scraping she finally squeezed her way in. She stood up to lanterns, music, laughter, dancing, drinking…then all got quiet. Goblin men and women, goblin boys and girls all stopped in their tracks and gawked up at Lessie.

"Don't be afraid, I won't hurt you." Lessie said, remembering all the books she had read, whenever something larger comes upon something smaller, this is the statement to proclaim. Silence. Then a low, grumbling voice called out, "Maybe *you* should be afraid. Maybe *we* will hurt *you*!" Lessie's heart jumped into her throat—this never happened in her novels She started to panic thinking how she could quickly escape. Then laughter rang out all around, the goblin she originally met laughed loudest of all. "The girl knows Adelaide!" Laughter turned into cheers and shouts, the music and dancing resumed. Lessie was shown to a stump, so she could sit and enjoy.

A lady goblin shoved a pint into Lessie's hand and gave her a wink. Lessie grimaced when she put it up to her mouth and politely set it down on the ground.

"I didn't know Miss Thor—Adelaide was so well known in the wood."

"Ah, she's a special breed she is," sighed one of the older goblins as he smoked his long pipe. "And she sure could dance!" The other goblin men laughed loudly. "Do you dance, sweetums?" They all laughed again and pushed Lessie into the midst of whirling goblins.

She stood there for a moment, looking around at the canopy of foliage above her, the fireflies that added festive luminescence, the joyful couples spinning around her. She couldn't help herself; she twirled and spun, laughed and sang. She danced with younger goblin men: Oak, Cedar, and Leif to name a few. She joined in and roared with laughter as the older goblin men drank so much, they stumbled around. She ogled as the goblin babies fell asleep in their mothers' arms. She lay down on a patch of velvety moss, the music slowed. A little snail was inching his way past her. She smiled, her eyes heavy.

The goblin she met in the wood, named Orion, pressed something into the palm of her hand. "Say hullo to Adelaide fer me."

Lessie jolted awake. To her surprise and confusion she was in her bed, in her room, in her house. She heard her baby brother crying, and Mama soothing him. The sun was glowing through her window. She blinked and rubbed her eyes. As she did, she heard a clink-clink like a coin being dropped to the floor. She looked down and that's exactly what it was. She picked it up and examined it, not recognizing it at first. Then it all came flooding back to her! She ran! Down the stairs, shoved on her shoes, they were still muddy, and threw on her coat, there was still a hole where it was ripped by the low branches. As she ran outside, she saw Adelaide Thorne peering out her window, smiling her big toothy smile. Lessie smiled back. Adelaide took a sip of her tea and moved out of sight of the window. Lessie focused on the wood. As she headed inside to find a chain for her own round, flat pendant she chuckled to herself.

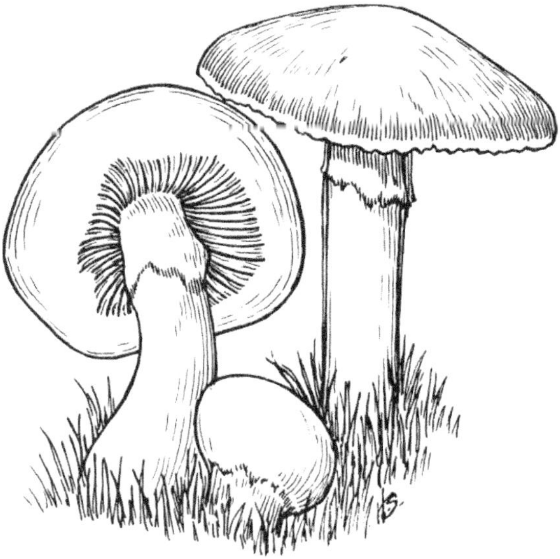

The Intelligence
... paulo da costa

Now that you've eaten the amanitas and stinkhorns in the forest and think that you can talk to me, let me tell you a six o'clock exclusive: I've been talking to you and yours since the sun began browning my kind. You've simply not been listening. Pardon me. A few of you have, but the majority have dismissed our followers as wackos with too much war paint on their faces and extravagant plumage on their heads.

Sure, I'm small and phallic. Even fallible. But I give wings to your mind so as to travel in universes you could have not dreamed on your own, I give light to those eyes of yours that are afraid of the darkness and make you believe that what you see is all the world is made of. We've been hinting at the blueprint of the universe for many cycles of extinction. You've thought our conversation a hallucination. No more than that. I know you've measured our brains against yours. It is not the size that matters.

We think in ways you can't yet imagine.

Keep this a secret. We're the messengers of the woods, forests and swamps. The trees' messenger pigeons.

If rational thought presupposes the ability to revise your beliefs, then it seems you failed. A creature of habit is not an intelligent being. You follow patterns and cravings and rivers just as the Tipipiuara rat follows the scent of nipookis. Mindlessly. To a trap. A predator's ambush.

Showing me your fancy smart watch? Smart about what? I see you have a thing for glitter. A watch that tells you where the sun is in the sky and where you are in the woods is certainly a miracle to admire. But is it more amazing than the Iguana Falls? It takes a certain kind of intelligence to be able to conjure up machines. To conjure up images from a cloud of nothing. I'll tell you what. I can sync up, too. What if I tell you that I also know exactly where I am at all times, I too have gone to the moon, would you believe it? So, what is the big deal? A rocket is not the only route to the moon.

If you're so intelligent, why are you coughing now? Most of my forests have burned away this summer. The river Tuautua no longer runs Guarinis. You can hardly breathe in this air. If you're so intelligent, how come you cannot stop these flames and their ire? Can you bring the air back to its crystalline sweetness?

Taking any last-minute bets on who's the intelligent one here?

There's no point in harbouring hard feelings since that's not going to give us a better brain. That's not going to give us a boat.

Let's just play cards. Cheat or Hearts?

You choose.

What pisses you off is not the charred forest. It's that you don't yet accept that your super intelligence has not gotten you out of this mess. You forgot that it's easier to destroy than to build. You are the child who broke the toy that seemed unbreakable, and now you can't fix it.

Your super intelligence will end up killing every last one of you. That will not be a bad thing. The problem is that you're also killing the rest of us. Sadly, that's what it means to be on the same boat. Even when there is no longer a river to sail it in.

Sure, I'm being prickly. The flames are loud. The smoke is deadly. We're both going to roast together at the edge of this almost dry river. Our flesh is sizzling already.

Smell it.

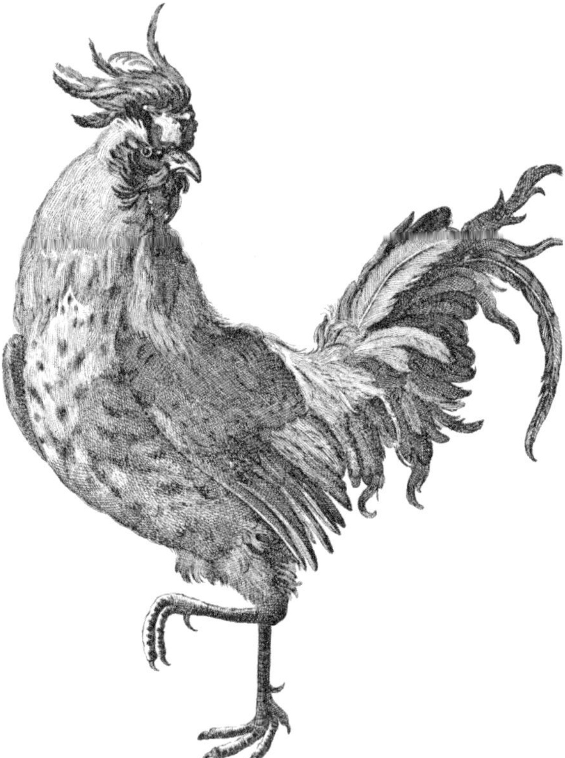

The Surprise Entrant
... Arvee Fantilagan

"What the hell is that!"

The pockets of chaos in the arena—of the hundred bloodthirsty middle-aged Filipinos cheering over cheap beer and cigars, of the booming announcements, and of the squawks and screeches and suffering interspersed among them — suddenly chorused in shock.

One of its regulars, the plump hairy Ganid, was waddling his way to the ring carrying a cage trailed by rainbows.

"That's incredible!" half of the crowd exclaimed.

"That's not fair!" the other half protested.

The referee in charge, who was also the event's emcee and bookkeeper, wanted to say the same thing. Nobody had ever entered a Sarimanok into a cockfighting tournament before!

Hell, nobody even knew Sarimanok existed for real. He'd only heard of the mythical chicken from his grandparents, themselves informed only by their own elders; of its rainbow feathers and golden crest and dazzling silhouettes, so elusive in their solitude in the forests of the Philippines that to even glimpse one was said to invite fortune for a lifetime.

The referee watched, mouth agape, as Ganid pulled the Sarimanok out from the cage, glittering and glistening, every bit as jaw-dropping as the fables had promised.

But, to his disappointment, it wasn't nearly as big as most of the other fighting birds in the arena. Ganid's scheduled opponent, Yabang, had a rooster twice its size: another gruff, unbeaten Brown Red gamefowl that he had bragged about importing straight from Japan. The Sarimanok didn't look aggressive, either; it wasn't trying to escape out of its owner's hands, not even cooing or clucking. It was simply craning its neck around, more like a curious dopey goat rather than an enraged warrior that was supposed to disembowel its opposition.

The referee felt a slight sting. Week in and week out, he presided over thrilling slugfests of roosters butchering each other for the entertainment of breeders and gamblers, but this one seemed too precious to get slaughtered just like most—especially on its very first cockfight.

"Okay," he sighed, "the Sarimanok can go, but the Brown Red can use a longer blade for its talons if Yabang wants to."

It was a huge advantage, but it didn't matter; nearly every bettor in attendance put their money on the newcomer, much to Yabang's irritation.

Its owner, Ganid, agreed with a grin. He, too, was that confident in the flashy feathery fowl that he discovered mingling with his poultry in his backyard last week.

The stories he'd heard were even more promising: about how fiercely a Sarimanok would protect its flock, beheading foes with a swipe of its claws, or punishing them with its full-throated, ear-piercing crows.

He was relieved he was able to tame it with just a few baits, worms, and brown grains, passive for now, but as soon as it felt threatened, they might as well go ahead and recycle its opponent into chicken soup—and crown Ganid a future millionaire.

"Do what you need to do, Sarimanok," he whispered to the radiant rooster as he brushed its flowing comb.

The cacophony in the stadium hushed to nervous anticipation; the only sounds remaining were those of other chickens clucking in their owner's hands as they waited for their turn to fight, or the grunts from Yabang's imported rooster, dour and impatient, already aroused for a bloody bout.

At the count of three, their owners tossed their fighters at each other.

"Fight!"

The Brown Red at once charged with ferocity, but the Sarimanok just gracefully flew past it and settled in the middle of the cockpit.

There, it threw its head back then belted out the most melodic crowing ever heard in that riotous venue. Rainbows erupted out of its beak, its wings, and its feathers; a prism's worth of colors beamed in all directions to the tune of everyone's awe.

Every bird present landed from midair or sprang out of their cages. They scampered in a hurry, not to fight but to feed, pecking at all the worms and bugs that were previously boisterous spectators and now helpless prey in their seats.

The Brown Red gamefowl, confused for a moment, lunged forward with talons braced for the kill. It landed behind the Sarimanok, pinning the plump hairy earthworm there that for so long had brought too many chickens into this slaughterhouse.

The Brown Red swallowed it in one slithery gulp.

Nearby were a millipede and a caterpillar that just a minute ago used to be a referee and an importer. Ever so slowly, they tried to crawl out of the cockpit, only to end up sliding in pieces down the throats of the other roosters that just joined the fray.

Throughout the now mostly empty arena was nothing but the peaceful sight of chickens prancing about, pecking and plucking, indulging in their unexpected feast.

They looked up to the ceiling. One by one, then two, then three at a time, and soon, in bone-rattling unison, they all belted their tiny mighty lungs out:

"Tik ti la okkk!"

The Sarimanok watched them atop a beam in the highest corner of the venue. With feathers shimmering in the sunlight, it crowed back:

"Tik ti la okkkk!"

Then it flapped out of an open window, rainbows tracing its flight like a feathered comet, headed for the next town with a cockfighting arena.

Amber and Jet
... Christa Bedwin

Crairata dabbed the tea bag on the too-white hem of her dress, again.

She had to redo this process over and over again. She darkened her dress with the tea, and as the days passed, it brightened up to white again. She had tried buying black dresses and brown and blue and green. It didn't matter. They all ended up white.

So, she dyed them with tea, just trying to make herself more acceptable. Less hard to look at.

It was her ugliest feature. She was too bright. She was too loud. She was too…alive. She talked too fast, and she thought too quickly compared to the others, and people hated that about her.

One day she decided to leave. Just. Leave. She took her warm cloak and a handful of nuts. She knew she would find enough leaves along her path to feed her fae little body. No need to overpack.

She hesitated a moment. Should she take crystals as a potential gift to share along her way?

No, she decided. This journey was for newness. When she carried crystals, she just worried constantly about how bright she made them glow, anyway. A nuisance. Her disability again.

She stopped in to say goodbye to her mother.

Instead of wishing her well or saying she'd miss her, her mom just fussed. "You're brighter than ever since you got back from the solstice gathering. Maybe I shouldn't have let you go."

Her mother dumped the entire house supply of tea bags in Crai's pouch. She hugged her fiercely, and said, over her shoulder, "I have done my best by you, love, but this is the only way I know how to help you fit in. Keep darkening yourself with the tea. I can't make you less bright or more quiet. All the goddesses know I have tried."

Those same familiar words, the ones that Crai could feel actually making her feel smaller. Shorter. Dimmer. Crai didn't argue with her mother, this time. She just nodded.

Once, when she had travelled to a market, Crai had met the most wonderful little brownie wearing sunglasses.

"Many of my people wear dark glasses when we leave home," she said, "because we're so used to being in the dark underground or inside trees. If we want to go outside, we need the shades."

The little brownie, whose name was Rea, hadn't minded Crai's brightness at all. Her sunglasses protected her.

Rea explained that the lenses in the glasses were made of two stones made of ancient tree sap, thinly sliced and polished. The darkest stone, deep and glossy as molasses, was jet. It was very dark, even totally black. The other stone, amber, was honey coloured, ranging from yellow to dark brown. *Not unlike my tea colour*, Crai though, and loved all the shades of all the lenses, from darkest black to lightest honey, immediately.

She didn't need to buy lenses for herself, of course. She could look at any light, even directly at the sun, without worry.

Later, she had wondered if she could have gifted a pair to her mother, maybe some more to her family, her neighbours. If they could see her through gentle amber lenses, would they be able to love her better? If they had their own filters to dim her light, would they see her with less rejection?

But, then, would they even try? Crai didn't feel sure at all that they would make the accommodation to put on glasses to love her better. They were so certain, so rigid in their perfect ideas on their crystal mountain. They didn't seem to feel any need to change their ways at all. According to them, it was only Crairata who should change herself to fit in better.

Crai's heart squeezed in her chest as she remembered how she had felt after her conversation with Rea at the market. It had been the first time she had let herself truly feel the injustice of her community's rejection. Somehow Rea's easy, unquestioning acceptance of her had cracked open all the pain she had been coping with all these years.

How lovely, how amazing and warm and easy it had been to talk to Rea. To feel her acceptance and total lack of question, rejection, or challenge.

It had made the stark reality of her own home life more obviously painful than ever.

Crai had been fascinated to learn about Rea's home in her tree and had asked her a lot of questions. The two had parted friends, hoping to visit each other…someday. It hadn't seemed likely at the time. But once the seed had been planted, it grew. Why not? Why not go find Rea and her tree?

Crai liked trees. They had such a lovely, gentle, welcoming hum. And trees liked light. They drank in sunshine and rain with equal thirst, never saying that one or the other was wrong. Crai had never experienced rejection from a tree.

She decided that she had dabbed enough brown on her dress for the journey. She would brighten as she went, but maybe, she hoped, when she arrived at Rea's trees, wouldn't need to darken herself anymore. Wouldn't that be amazing? If she blended in well enough in the trees with tree people?

Crai vaguely had the idea that Rea lived toward the mountains, from the market town where she had met her. Crai walked to the market town and stayed for the night. Happily, the tavern owner knew Rea and drew Crai a map to Rea's village.

Crai arrived by evening, before sun set, foot-sore but happy. Rea saw her right away and ran down the main path to jump into her arms. Crai wouldn't have guessed her mushroom-shaped little friend would be able to jump so well, but she was not heavy, and Crai hugged her tight.

"Crai! My little sperm whale!" Rea greeted her.

A laugh sputtered out of Crai. "That's the first thing you say when you see me? What do you mean?"

"Well, I have been thinking about the super-powers you told me about, how you are the brightest and loudest in your family. Sperm whales are the loudest animals on earth. They can make two hundred and thirty decibels of noise. It's loud enough to act like x-ray radar on any beings they find in the dark."

Other villagers, all wearing dark glasses too, were gathering around. "Wow, that's even better than bats' ability to see in the dark," said one.

"Awesome," echoed another.

"I am not loud all the time," Crai protested. The goddesses all knew how hard she had worked on herself to learn to speak more quietly, more moderately. She hadn't been able to dim her light without tea bags, but she had learned to speak more quietly. Usually.

"That's even better," said another. "Superpowers you can control." The others murmured comfortable sound of agreement.

"We have all been making special dark glasses in case you came," said a little one. "Now you are here, we can try them out in the gathering room."

"Yes, yes!" chorused the others, and Crai found herself carried along with the little swarm of brownies into a nearby tree. Rea had not given up her position, hugged to Crai's chest as she was. Crai didn't mind. It felt good. Like they belonged together.

As the creatures bustled into the gathering hall inside the tree, they switched their outdoor glasses for new pairs hanging at the door.

They sat down and all gazed at Crai. "Beautiful," she heard some of the older one's murmur.

"Very beautiful," said some younger ones sitting behind the old ones, and Crai blushed. She had never been stared at for so long before without people looking away in disgust at her brightness.

"We found a way to cut the lenses thinner, so we can see indoors and still see you," explained Rea.

Crai felt a huge ball of some emotion surge up in her chest, so that she felt that she might explode. They had invented special lenses just to accommodate her?

She set Rea down for safety, as she was not used to this feeling in her body and did not know what might happen.

A trio of elder brownies approached Crai. "While we were making the new lenses, we also made you a belt of amber and jet, our two tree stones, to welcome you."

Crai picked up Rea and set her down on her own two feet, and the other brownies reached up to clasp the beautiful belt of amber and jet discs around her waist.

"With these stones from the ancient blood of our trees, we want you to know that from now on, wherever you roam, you always belong with us. You now have roots here. We love the illumination you bring to us. None of us have that and your difference is precious."

"But we hope you don't roam too far any time soon," Rea said. "Wouldn't you like to come and have a cup of tea?"

Yes, indeed. A warm cup of tea and a cozy chat with her friend were exactly what Crai wanted most in the world right now, she thought. The weight of the amber and jet discs around her waist felt delicious, a weight of belonging. A grounding.

Just what she had most hoped for.

No Matter the Cost
... Meghan Victoria

Avery Stone would have rather had her eyes pecked from her skull than listen to the man beside her. At least the pain of a sharp beak would have focused her senses instead of dulling them to the point of death. She drummed her fingernails against the table and scanned the lawns of Unger's estate. The vows had been exchanged, the champagne guzzled, the bindings set. The guests had side-eyed the gown she'd found in the back racks of a thrift shop, Unger had presided over the ceremony with a sage glint in his eye, and her new husband had clung to their one-sided conversation with more enthusiasm than a lake leech.

Weddings, it turned out, were obnoxious affairs—even one as small and necessary as hers.

Despite the gauzy décor, Birchwood was as she remembered, though it had been nearly a year. That had been their deal, she and Unger. Their deal, and his sacrifice. *Go, see the world, before you hunker down and become a cankerous old codger like me.* He'd raised her since she'd been little more than a tadpole, since he'd found her half-feral and wandering the tangled wood that surrounded Birchwood's crumbling walls. She loved him with every beat of her fickle, greedy heart, and so she'd heeded his advice.

She wondered if he'd suspected, all those months ago, that she wouldn't return alone. If that, too, had been part of his sacrifice. Unger understood the price of keeping their forged family together better than anyone.

Avery swirled her untouched champagne and wondered if stabbing her new husband's hand with a fork would make her feel less claustrophobic when a flash of sparkle caught her eye. A slim figure in an ostentatious dress slipped through the back gates and towards the forest beyond.

Bess.

Avery looked for Unger's balding head, but he'd disappeared as soon as the meat skewers had run out. She sighed. She'd been avoiding this argument since she'd returned home, since Bess had taken one look at her husband-to-be and began sharpening her knives.

Avery pushed away the champagne and stood, muttering something about the washroom. She doubted he noticed, his story suffering not a hitch or change in tone as she moved from the table, tossing a final glance over her shoulder as she crept through the gates, across the clearing and into the wood.

Far from the light of sparklers and candles, the forest lay simmering beneath the last rays of sunset. It was old, its trees gnarled and twisted, wizard's beard drifting in the breeze.

"Hello, dear friends," Avery whispered, trailing her fingers along bark. The trees didn't part for her, but rather crowded close, catching their branches in her hair, snagging her dress, coaxing her to shed her shoes. As her bare feet sunk into the moss strewn earth, she let herself smile her first real smile of the evening.

Too long too long too long, the trees chorused in the wind.

Yes. It had been too long indeed.

The air turned damp and rich as Avery wandered deeper into the forest's embrace. She'd always taken solace in the small, quiet things. A mushroom nestled into a knotted trunk, the precision of insects crawling over a fresh corpse. She liked the dark unknown, the thrill of not knowing what might be lurking around a blind corner. Although she felt altogether unprepared for where this particular blind corner might take her.

"I can hear you there," a low voice said from the growing darkness.

Avery stepped through a small gap in the trees. Bess sat in a mossy hollow, looking like a beam of moonlight against the dirt of the forest floor. Her features were sharp beneath her wave of silver hair, freckles glittering like stardust, drawing Avery's gaze to the small, white scar marring her right cheekbone. But it was her eyes, too big, too green, too knowing, that always caught Avery's attention and refused to let go.

"Well aren't you sparkly tonight," Avery murmured, mouth dryer than a splintering log as she eyed the diamond studded clip that clung precariously in Bess's hair.

Bess laughed her rocksalt rasp. "I think you're lost, Goblin Heart," she said. "There's nothing sparkly to be found in these parts."

Avery fiddled with the small green gem that dangled from her necklace. She'd once asked Bess about the nickname. Bess had grinned her dimpled smile and said that Avery's heart was greedy as a goblin's, that those she claimed as her own, she refused to let go.

Bess wasn't wrong. And now they were here.

Avery sank slowly to sit amongst the roots of her favorite dogwood. The trees rustled. *Mine, mine, mine.* Dirt clung to the white of her dress, reclaiming her.

"Why didn't you tell me?" Bess asked finally, when Avery thought she might choke on the silence.

Avery's fingers stilled against her necklace. "Because you would have tried to stop me."

She hadn't been sure what she meant to do, when she left a year ago. Between Unger's coaxing and the tug of her sacrifice, her path had been clear even if her head had been filled with fog.

"Or I could have helped you go about it the right way," Bess said. "Without this farce of a wedding. It wouldn't have taken much to lure a stranger down into the woods for the sacrifice, Ave."

"The wedding isn't a farce, Bess. It *is* the sacrifice."

And there it was. Avery watched the flicker of emotions cascade over Bess's pale features, too quick for most to catch. But Avery knew Bess better than the air in her lungs, and every expression felt like a splinter to her heart.

Bess's sparkle stuttered. "No." Waves of silver cascaded over her shoulders as she shook her head. "Killing this idiot is the sacrifice."

Avery sighed and tracked the path of a beetle as it scuttled over her fingers. "Killing a man I care nothing for is hardly a sacrifice."

"Of course it is, you stupid cow. It's a sacrifice of your innocence."

"My innocence isn't the price," Avery said quietly, digging her fingers into the earth and refusing to meet Bess's gaze.

They'd never put words to this *thing* between them. Bess had always been fire and passion, prone to grand gestures and impulsiveness. Avery had been overwhelmed and more than a little awestruck when she had tumbled into her life, blazing like a comet. While Unger had dreamed the daughter he'd longed for into being from the earthy forest depths, Avery had plucked the companion of her heart from the sky itself. She'd long wondered what she'd done to pique the interest of a star. Wishes only worked, after all, if something wished back.

"If not your innocence, then what?" Bess demanded.

Avery's smile was a sad, wan thing as she looked up. "My heart."

The magic of wishing required something in exchange. Unger's price for claiming the daughter he'd long coveted was sending her away without knowing if she would return. Avery's price for finding the companion of her heart was to give herself to another. Cruel, but the world required balance. Avery wouldn't trade her wish for anything, even knowing the sacrifice it demanded.

Bess's glow flared against the night. "Your bleeding goblin heart belongs to *me*."

"Bess—" Avery began, but Bess didn't let her finish, standing to shake out the edges of her dress.

"I'm taking care of this." Bess's light dimmed to embers as she backed away.

"Bess!" Avery lunged for her arm, but Bess was as much part of the night as Avery was of the earth.

Her fingers grasped air, and only the chirp of crickets answered her call.

The trees rustled. A figure emerged at her side.

"Let her go," Unger said, his hand heavy on her shoulder.

The top of his head came barely to Avery's nose, but his presence wrapped around her, as familiar and comforting as the forest itself.

"She's going to do something drastic," Avery said.

"Most likely."

"Unger." Avery shook herself free of his hand and turned to face him. "A sacrifice must be made for every wish granted. You know that as well as I."

He nodded gravely. "The sacrifice has been made."

"And Bess will *unmake* it."

Unger reached out and took her hands. "A sacrifice is only unmade if you entered into it with no intention to uphold your part of the bargain." Trust Unger to skirt about in the grey areas, where the light couldn't quite reach. He squeezed her fingers. "We do what is necessary to keep this family together."

Branches stroked her skin, rattling their agreement. *Ours ours ours.*

Avery sighed. "No matter the cost."

"No matter the cost," Unger agreed.

Through the trees, silver light sparked, growing hotter and brighter until Avery threw an arm over her eyes. Screams pierced the night. The forest shuddered.

And then, silence.

Avery gripped Unger's arm.

No matter the cost.

Dirty Girl
... Sarah L. Pratt

Goblin Mode

Oxford English Dictionary Word of the Year, 2022
Definition: behaviour which is unapologetically self-indulgent, lazy, slovenly, or greedy, typically in a way that rejects social norms or expectations.

LiveRoom.com/LR/DickNet/

go_Gnome_rgo_Home (moderator): Greetings digital Dicks. I finally have an update on the puzzling disappearance of FunZEEo creator Shiny Penny. To recap, Penny was allegedly one of the most popular beauty influencers on the video platform, with (alleged) sponsorships from e.l.f. cosmetics, La Roche-Posay skin care, and SKIMS shapewear. Even I'd heard of her, and when I think foundation I think concrete, not concealer. Point being, this girl was a Brad Mondo level internet celebrity, and then she was just…gone.

At first, I thought to file this in the Jenna Marbles bucket of clayfooted digital gods, but after a thorough search of even the crustiest folds of the world wide web, I realized this wasn't a case of withdrawal from public life due to a racist/transphobic gaffe, no outing as an antivaxxer. Nothing, and I mean no thing. This girl didn't just vanish, she'd been erased. No socials, no tags, no mentions, and no wayback.

I was ready to chalk it up to a seriously profesh fix job for a wealthy young woman grown weary of parasocial media. And remember netizens, we don't pry into people's RLs. Cyberspace is our investigative domain, and if the mystery can't be solved within those parameters, it's not a case for the Dicks.

In this instance, it seemed the net wasn't going to tell on itself, but then I received a DM from an LR/Beauty thread mod claiming to have transcripts from Penny's last few uploads. I cannot vouch for their veracity, but I'm posting them here in the hope that our sleuths can glean some clues.

<u>VIDEO 1</u>

Hey, y'all! You know I love, love, love trying new brands, and I'm soooo excited to share my latest haul with you, a company I've literally never heard of but am fucking obsessed with already. Seriously, you heard it here first. DIRT beauty.

Today I'm gonna talk about their eye pencils for all my smoked out witches, batwing bitches, and liquid liner QUEENS. This is the product you've been fiending for your whole life. And y'all know there is no greater test of a liner than my little hooded eye, so I'm just gonna apply it now…this shade is chanterelle…but it comes in like ten delicious earthy tones. See how that wing just draws itself? Wears all day and maybe longer, but I'm a religious instep skincare girly—shout out to garage pussy!—so y'all can let me know.

Eek! So gorgeous, I am ultra obsessed. Seriously, DIRT Beauty, I love you, and y'all are not gonna want to sleep on these pencils. Check out part 2 for their bronzer. Byeeeeiii!

<u>4 Replies</u>

TrenchDaddy284: UGH, I wanna try this liner so bad and I'm getting zero (non-porn) search results for DIRT.

Booze_Clues: Hey Trench, maybe head over to LR/Beauty and don't derail our investigation?

NancyBoyz: Um, they just said they can't find DIRT on the internet. I'd call that a clue. Gnome, have we considered that this is a hoax?

go_Gnome_rgo_Home (moderator): Certainly, but we know she existed, and she does appear to be missing, if only from the internet.

<u>VIDEO 2</u>

So the liner lasts like, way longer than a day. Kinda loving it though. So much that I went to bed last night without doing my garage pussy. Didn't brush my teeth or put in my nightguard either. Best. Sleep. Ever.

Anyway, I promised bronzer next. And before you call me out, I'm having a puffy period day and skipped the skims. For real, it feels great bleeding into an old pair of Hanes, and not having KK's g-string splitting my cooch in half.

So the bronzer comes in two shades, Clay and, uh…Arbutus Bark.

Hmm, looks like dirt. When was the last time I got dirty, like, with actual dirt? Just blending it out now…still looks kinda muddy. But loving this snatched grimecore look for me, might take a walk in the forest behind my house. Check out part 3 for DIRT Beauty lip oil.

2 Replies

NancyBoyz: Loving the craptions!

go_Gnome_rgo_Home (moderator): Indeed, though my research produced no evidence of partnerships with La Roche-Posay, SKIMS, or e.l.f.

Booze_Clues: Her house backs onto a forest. Anyone know what area she lives in?

VIDEO 3

Not a makeup vid, just an update while I eat beef jerky in bed—shout out to McSweeney's! 10/10 would recommend. Nom, nom... Anyway, some folks have left comments asking if I'm okay, that I look like I'm not taking care of myself. I'll be real, my last everything shower is a distant memory, so I'm gonna take a couple weeks off creating content for a little self-care. Love y'all, and I'll see you soon. Byeeeiii!

4 Replies

TrenchDaddy284: She sounds fun. I wouldn't kick her out of bed for eating jerky

Booze_Clues: FFS, can you not?

TrenchDaddy284: Stop downvoting me, Booze. You have no sense of humour.

NancyBoyz: McSweeney's is a Canadian brand, right?

VIDEO 4

I'm BAAAACK! Bed rotting since the last video, and it is fucking awesome. I wanna welcome my new followers, including the guy who asked when I last changed my panties, and the answer is I don't remember. Want me to mail 'em to you, ya bird?

Catching you up on the latest. Skims terminated our contract, so I literally lit my whole collection on fire. Who needs a second set of nipples? Haven't heard from elf, which I still love, even if I'm on this DIRT kick. *loud belching* Annnd I've been eating a lot of ice cream. Turns out I'm lactose intolerant as ever, but I discovered something phenomenal. Not. Holding. It. In. And you don't need a twitchy tummy to benefit from this practice. I'm so serious.

BTW, that DIRT bronzer lives up to its long wearing promise. I look like a racially insensitive casting from the Hollywood golden age.

Back with a new video real soon. Love you, byeeeiii!

7 Replies

Booze_Clues: Well that solves it, a couple weeks without creating content and the internet decides you never existed.

go_Gnome_rgo_Home (moderator): Haha, Booze. Just keep in mind we have no way of actually knowing how much time is passing between these vids.

Booze_Clues: The hell, Trench? A downvote?

TrenchDaddy284: FWIW I did laugh at your joke

Detective_91753: Hello Dear! Would you like to make 10K a month wokring from home?

Booze_Clues: Gnome?

go_Gnome_rgo_Home: Blocked. Post stays though, for posterity.

VIDEO 5

Finally left the bed! I'm in the woods behind my house, and my hair is wet because there's a pond here. Like, I didn't even know! So, being in dire need of a bath, I went skinny dipping.

Before you ask, yes, it's really me, Shiny Penny. No makeup, no filter, no halo light. My roots are showing, and the pits and bits haven't seen a razor in forever. Giving up, right? Wrong! I'm giving back. To me! I've had time to think, to rest, to explore this super cute forest on my own property that I bought with all that sweet garage pussy cash.

I'm fucking happy y'all, and I'm not gonna gatekeep my secret to good vibes. I love all my followers, but this one's for the girlies. I'm telling you, grow a bush, get dirty, wear big comfy clothes, eat tacos in bed, and fart whenever you want to.

Seriously, I've never felt more beautiful. Fuck the lip oil.

3 Replies

NancyBoyz: Wow… I hope she's okay. #MentalHealth

TrenchDaddy284: What do you mean mental health? Masterclass in how to tank your brand, sure, but that doesn't mean she's crazy.

NancyBoyz: Okay, but her behaviour seems pretty out there.

TrenchDaddy284: Would you say that about a guy who didn't wash his hair for a few days?

Booze_Clues: Forest with a pond. Probably rural-ish. Acreage? And we think she might be Canadian? If we could narrow it down, Google Earth might turn something up.

SCREENSHOT 1

go_Gnome_rgo_Home (moderator): Allegedly taken minutes after that last video went live, before the account disappeared entirely.

Shiny Penny
Beauty is LIFE!!!
10.8M Followers

This account has been suspended due to violent and/or disturbing content.

6 Replies

TrenchDaddy284: TF? Did we miss something?

NancyBoyz: Something violent and disturbing?

Booze_Clues: FunZEEo *is* owned by a Russian Oligarch. But I still say hoax.

AgathaAmnesia: Late to the party, but this is a fascinating case. I used to follow Penny, and I'm shocked that the disappearance of a pretty white girl isn't making more waves.

NancyBoyz: Welcome, Ag. And Trench will downvote me for this, but it bears mentioning that she likely wasn't so pretty at the end, was she?

go_Gnome_rgo_Home (moderator): If not a hoax it's one of the most thorough cases of internet erasure I've ever seen. Or perhaps something like the Mandela effect? A beautiful woman decaying before the eyes of millions. And then…the Penny vanishes.

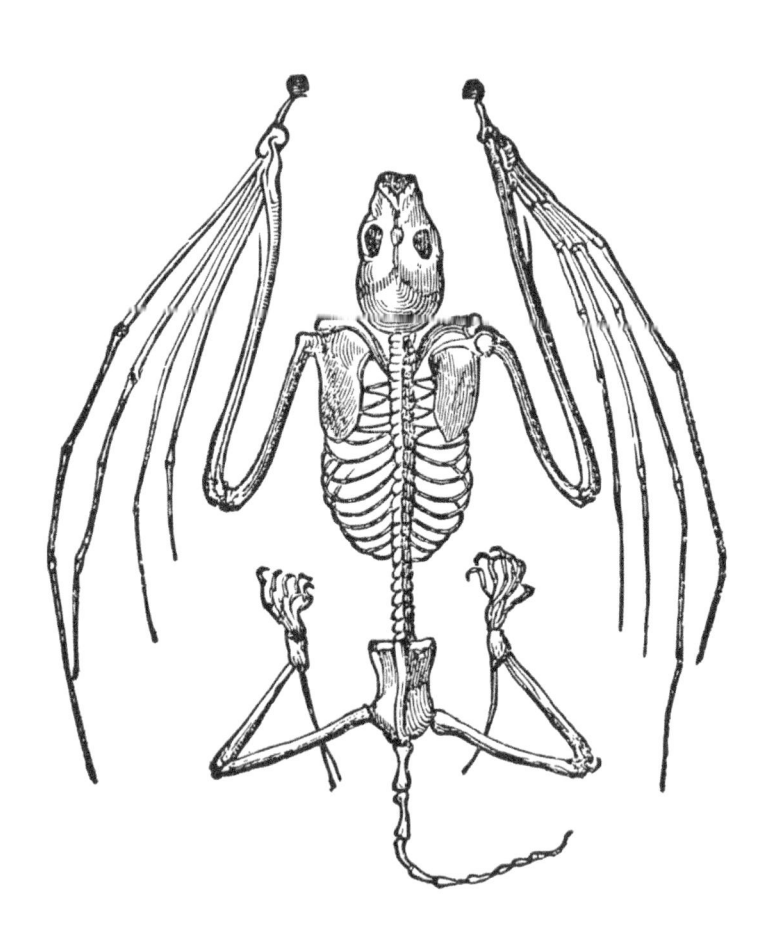

Sacrifices
... Jason Ellis

In the morning, before the first coffee has been drunk, I check the skull to see what work has been done. It is in the backyard under a tarp weighted down at the edges by broken cinder blocks and stones I dragged up from the creek. The world is fresh and dewy, and the grass stains my work boots dark. Carefully, I remove each stone, and then roll the tarp back to see. Beneath, the grass has grown pale and sun-starved in the tarp-shaped patch, but at the center where I removed some of the grass to expose the soil, lay the skull. I believe it is a fox, though it is possible it could be a cat.

I found it on one of my walks, still fresh but in bad shape. Just the skull, nothing more, but otherwise intact. This happens. Usually, I just find interesting rocks to carry back, but sometimes I find bones of some sort. Occasionally a skull. I have mounted most of them. Look closely, around my cozy home and you are likely to spot a few in the garden amongst the flowers, mounted to a shed well. Hung on a tree.

I imagine under the tarp each night how the beetles and grubs come out to pick and chew through cartilage, sinew, and muscle, imagine the little lives that squish and crawl around the once-brainpan. With each new morning for almost a month now, a little more bone has been cleared bit by bit away. It is almost complete now. I pick it up and shake it, listening for the rattle of its diminishing innards.

On the breeze, a flurry of my several windchimes jangle and thunk from the front yard, and I am struck by their dissonance. The glassy jangle—my little house, all yellow and heavily adorned both in and out with careful collection and curation with what others might call clutter. The hollow thunk—this pocket world, my yard, filled with the rocks, bones, and wondrous garden of plants, loamy and rich. I marvel at the circular nature of it; the organic accretion of my life stuff as counterpoint to the organic hollowing of the skull. I feel humble and thankful in the presence of the order and entropy, the cosmic drama writ both small and large all around me.

I notice in the night a huddle of puffballs has grown up suddenly around a rotting branch, as they do, forming a rough fairy ring.

Somewhere distant, a rooster crows, and I consider if I should get chickens.

Then, with a rude thump, a car door slams shut.

🍄

"You have a dead bat on your porch," the man says as I round the corner of the house.

"Can I help you?" I ask.

He wears a uniform and looks vaguely like a delivery man, with "David" written in red cursive on his upper right chest. I see no deliveries in his hands, though he holds a clipboard. He looks tidy. On the other hand, I must seem like the witch of some modern-day wilds to him; a mad, feral soul in dirty overalls and morning hair.

"You have a dead bat there," he repeats. "You should clean it up. It's unsanitary. And the ants are getting at it; you'll have them inside soon, too."

I chuckle. "I probably already do have them inside," I say, taking out my phone, and snapping a picture of the bat.

"Why did you take a picture of it?"

I shrug. "I've taken a picture of it every day since my cat left it."

"But why?" he asked again.

I blow a tassel of hair out from my eyes. "Why did she leave it? Or why did I take a picture?"

He says nothing, but I can see in his eyes he thinks I am daft. "I don't know. Both?"

"It's nothing too remarkable," I say. "Priss leaves me sacrifices because she loves me and understands fairness. I took the picture because … I don't know. Just to see what happens, I guess."

He nods like he understands completely, and I choose not to explain any further. The awkwardness pools around us damply… His eyes survey my yard, my gardens. Old farm equipment turned rusty lawn ornament. The shaggy grass. Bird feeders haphazardly hung and strewn about. For a moment, I feel… shame? What would he wonder if he saw the inside, I think? The shelves and tables of my bric-a-brac, my knick-knacks. And oh, the stacks and stacks of books.

After a moment, he resets the conversation with, "Right. Okay. Anyway, I'm sorry to bother you but I'm Dave with

PestGuard. We're in your area letting people know about the Fall specials we're running right now."

"PestGuard?" I ask.

"Yeah," he adds, nodding toward his van. "We exterminate. Termites, ants. Most bugs, really."

"Uh huh."

"Are you the homeowner?"

"Yup." I lean against the door frame. I was wrong. Dave is not really a man yet. I am surprised he introduced himself as Dave and not David as his nametag reads. He carries himself wrong; too young, awkward, to have grown into a one-syllable name like Dave with all the middle-aged male swagger that it implies.

"Oh, ok. Great. Well, anyway PestGuard has some specials right now that some of your neighbors in the area have been taking advantage of. They're protecting their property and homes by having us out to spray quarterly." He looks down at his clipboard. "We only have a few slots still available. Uh, the Ronsons already signed up today, and the Stephensons are thinking about it. Do you, uh, know them?"

I point at the trees all around us. My land is small, but the trees enclose it, make it feel more remote than it is. "Afraid not," I say. "I don't know my neighbors much." This is a lie. I do know my neighbors well. I also know that no one named Ronson or Stephenson lives anywhere near us.

"Ah, well, there's been a lot of interest in the specials lately. Especially this time of year with Fall coming soon. A lot of bugs try to get indoors when the weather turns cooler."

I grunt an acknowledgement. "But we like bugs here."

He seems surprised by this. "You do? Having the bugs here will attract other types of things though too… like spiders."

"But we like spiders here too," I reply.

He looks at me blankly. Is it because he is so far off script? Or is it because no one has ever responded to him this way before. I believe it is the latter.

"I guess then…," he stutters. "I guess there's really nothing you need from PestGuard then, is there?"

"Nope," I say.

He thanks me for my time and scutters down the porch steps with his clipboard, then down the sidewalk to the drive. At the crepe myrtle, all alive in crimson, he pauses to inspect something.

After a moment he turns back to me and yells, "Your tree has bag worms." He pauses for me to respond; when none comes, he adds, "We can help with those too."

"Vinegar and neem oil!" I yell back in response.

He nods his head back and raises his hand to me in farewell, dreamily. I wave back. "Okay then," he says, as he climbs into his van. He marks something down on his clipboard, starts the engine, and backs away. At my ankle, I feel something rubbing and look down to see Priss. I pet her, my hand starting at her ears, rubbing down her tabby back, and stopping at the base of her tail.

"Mrrraow," she says.

I place my hand under her belly and lift her up into my arms. When I look up, the PestGuard van has slipped behind the veil of trees just beyond my view, and we are alone again.

I climb the steps to find that Priss has left me another sacrifice—this time a chipmunk—in another spot nearby on the porch. I wonder how Dave noticed the bat and not the chipmunk, but then it makes sense to me. People like him only see the most obvious things. That would be a tidy way to live, I think. An uncomplicated life, but also a minimal one. What value is a life, I wonder, spent living tidily? Minimally? I think of the skull, under the tarp again in the backyard. Even in death it is robust, not at all minimal. And when the bugs are done with their work, I will honor it by including it in my world here where it will not be at all tidy in the slightest.

My stomach rumbles. Coffee and toast sound right, so I turn to go inside. "How about some food for you too?" I ask Priss. She mrrraows again, huskily.

"Good girl," I tell her, confident that everything is as it should be.

Tomorrow, maybe, I will get chickens.

Seasons
... Nik Kuipers

There are soft red and yellow leaves in your face, in your hair, at your fingertips. White branches poke into your thighs and snag your sweater. You feel acorns brush your cheeks: rusty, bumpy, and soft, with brown stems so delicate that with one twist they tear, and the breeze catches them, and they go down, *thunk, thunk, thunking* through branches, the sound echoing between trees and landing with a soft *plop* in the grave of leaves and acorns beneath you.

Your face is lifted towards a sharp sky. The loamy spice emanating from the earth dissipates and up here the air is instead scented with clouds, and the fading warmth of summer sun, and a faint, snowy chill.

There's silence except for the rustle of leaves; are the cicadas and frogs sleeping, or have they started an early hibernation? A bird will call out, but the sound is snatched quickly by the breeze somewhere (or some*time*) else. Now, the gray bones creeping from the red and gold and brown leaves are replacing the noise with warnings of winter.

There's weight on your neck, a heaviness that can't quite be pinpointed. And there's a wetness seeping through your clothes, staining the air with a darker smell than autumn spice. And your hair keeps getting in your mouth, which you can't seem to close. And in your eyes, which refuse to blink. There are little white things, and little black things, and they crawl all over you. Unexpected fizzing brings life to your very skin, dissipating it into weathered and gnarled patches. Yet you keep still, for some reason—so still—except sometimes when the breeze catches you and threatens to send you to the ground like an acorn. Somehow these things don't affect you as they used to. If you could, you would wonder why, or even how. But you can't, and you don't.

Leaves spiral toward the ground. There is water beading on the now bare branches that first freezes and melts, but then stays frozen. The sky is a thousand slate colored obsidian daggers; gusts of wind slicing through your hair, through your bones, sharper than any blade. Through you, directly to the heart of the tree you rest against. The cold rests within you, locks up your joints, curls your fingers into unintentional fists, as though you are angry for not being able to feel anything. But you aren't angry at all.

The silence grows deeper. It grows inside of you, too. Your clothes hang in shreds, pieces ripped away with the wind or by curious birds. Your joints can no longer lock. You're on the ground now as well as in the trees, nestled among the crunchy leaves and acorns. The wind cuts through high in the treetops, yet in some places on the ground leaves have blown over you, or trees stand guard, and they block the worst of it.

Delicate flakes of snow soon follow. They pile all around, bitter cold, yet you remain, and the beauty of the trees topped with the white lace brings you no awe.

Eventually the sky breaks, and sun shoots down through the branches. Weak sun, but the water beading on branches freezes less and less often, and then not at all, and the snow melts into rivulets so the forest becomes a river instead. There's always water flooding across you, or dripping onto you, or floating you somewhere else entirely. But you have no attachment to any single state or location.

At night, the wind kicks up, howling fiercely, and bangs what remains of you in the trees against their trunks, scraping their own bark like you might cure them of their sentience. You make a hollow sound that's swallowed in the clamor of the wind. But you have no need to be heard, or to cure any living thing.

Now the constant wetness has mugged the wind into giving up its bitterness. Knurled red buds blunt the pale branches, and there's a reddish purple haze as if someone spray painted a canopy. The breeze smells almost salty, like the ocean. You have not regained desire or regret, but you feel the return of the unexpected in the cracks that the winter, at the depths of its cruelty, froze into you. Fizzing becomes a pulse, and then spores: yellow and orange and red, organic shapes like the clouds in a sunset all melting together. Connection sparks, taking more of you with it.

All at once the green springs forward. The gray retreats. Bugs swarm the air and birds mass in the treetops, above you and around you. There is no longer silence, there is no longer cold, not for a long while. You are a part of it all now. The season will change again, and you will too. But this time, with the rest of the living forest, you will be able to wonder.

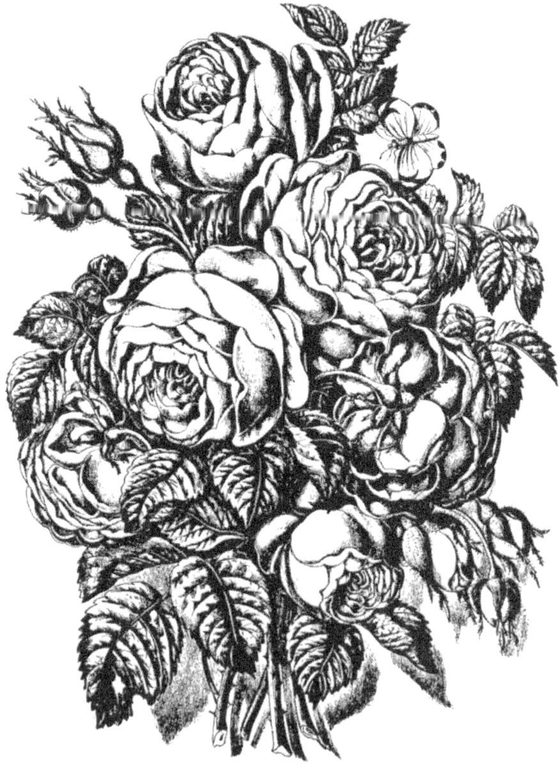

About the Authors

Cordelia Kelly

Cordelia Kelly is the author of the Port of Lost Souls series and YA fantasy novel *The Sibyl and the Thief*. Her short stories have been published in horror anthologies, including "Herbalista" in *Prairie Witch* and "Dare to Survive" in *Dark & Stormy*. She has released a collection of horror shorts called Then She Said Hush, which includes her post-apocalyptic story "Unfreeze" which won first place in fiction at the 2019 Geneva Literary Prizes. She spends her free time learning digital illustration and writing recaps of R.L. Stine's *Fear Street* books on her blog Shadyside Snark.

Margaret Campbell

Margaret is a career copywriter sick to death of using language primarily for search engine optimization. As a creative writer, she is most interested in literary genre fiction, genre poetry, and telling stories about people on the outside, whether or not they are bothering to look in.

Kim Claussen

Kim Claussen (she/her) is a neurodivergent author, exploring mostly speculative fiction genres with a focus on adventure and escapism (such as fantasy, sci-fi, urban fantasy, romance, romantasy…). Her works explore themes of magic, self-worth, and found family dynamics. When not writing, she can be found devouring other works of fiction of various mediums, playing D&D with friends and family, and chasing down her energetic golden retriever. *Goblincore* is her first publication.

Lareina Abbott

Lareina Abbott pens Métis themed speculative fiction, essays and memoir. Her stories have a tie to the spiritual or natural world, and to ancestry. She received the Writers Guild of Alberta 2023 Howard O'Hagan award for her short story "Ma Soeur Marie" published in the *Prairie Witch* anthology, and is an alumni of the Audible Indigenous Writers Circle. She is a member of the Métis Nation of Alberta and her family names are Huppé, Desjarlais, and Cyr. She originates from a cattle ranch in northern British Columbia but currently lives and writes in Calgary/Mokinstsis on MNA District 5 and Treaty 7 territory. She is on Instagram at @boneblackstories.

Calvin D. Jim

Nominated multiple times for the Prix-Aurora Award, Calvin D. Jim is a Calgary lawyer-turned-writer whose Asian-inspired tales have appeared in numerous anthologies and publications. He also writes articles on Japanese mythology for a Calgary-based Japanese-Canadian community association A self-proclaimed geek, he managed to wrangle his wife and two sons into board games and Karate (not necessarily in that order, and not without injury).

Ash Vale

Ash Vale (they/them) is a queer, non-binary, neurodivergent Canadian. They're a big fan of cryptids, guts, weird li'l guys, and cats. You can find their newsletter and stories at https://linktr.ee/ashvale or find them on most social media as @AshValeWrites.

J.A. Renwick

Jessica Renwick dove into the world of writing fiction as a preteen and never looked back. Naturally, this led to a career as a library assistant, and her first middle-grade book, *The Book of Chaos*, was published in 2018. Her middle-grade horror novel, *Ghosts of Gastown*, is coming out in October 2024 with the Yellow Dog imprint of Great Plains Press. She lives with her partner, two dogs, and a flock of backyard chickens in Red Deer, Alberta. You can find her online at www.jessicarenwickauthor.com

Alex Benarzi

Alex is a writer, editor, and educator in Calgary, AB. He is fascinated by the little absurdities that colour our world. Alex is also passionate about accessibility in the literary industry. Alex's short stories and flash fiction have appeared in Coffin Hop Press, The Selkie, Seventh Terrace, and Prairie Soul Press. Alex edited the When Words Collide 2024 anthology, War of the Words.

Joseph Halden & Rhonda Parrish

Joseph and Rhonda enjoy getting together and telling stories whether they be in roleplaying games, poems or flash fiction. This is their first time collaborating on the latter.

Robert Fields Byrne

Rob Fields Byrne is an American writer and musician living in Chicago, Illinois.

Valerie Hunter

Valerie Hunter teaches high school English and has an MFA in writing for children and young adults from Vermont College of Fine Arts. Her stories have appeared in publications including Beneath Ceaseless Skies, Capsule Stories, OFIC, and Sonder, as well as multiple anthologies.

A.J. McCutchen

I'm just a guy who spends a lot of time living and sometimes I like to write about it.

Brent Nichols

Brent Nichols is a fantasy, science fiction, and crime writer, bon vivant, and man about town. He likes good beer, bad puns, high adventure and low comedy. He's never been seen in the same room as Batman, but that's probably just a coincidence. He's the author of End of the Loop, available wherever gritty crime novels and psychological thrillers are sold.

Emily A. Grigsby

Emily A. Grigsby lives in Ohio, USA and is a stay-at-home wife & homeschooling mom of three. She has always been a fan of fantasy fiction but has mild aphantasia which inhibits her ability to visualize. She loves looking at pictures while reading to help with this. She also is a person who stutters (PWS) but doesn't let this hold her back. She is a born-again Christian and is very involved in her church.

paulo da costa

Born in Angola, and raised in Portugal, paulo da costa is a writer, editor and translator living in the Rocky Mountains of Canada. He is thrice the recipient of the 2024, 2023 and 2020 Alberta Writers' Guild James H. Gray Award for Short Nonfiction, the 2003 Commonwealth First Book Prize for the Canada-Caribbean Region, the W. O. Mitchell City of Calgary Book Prize and the Canongate Prize for short-fiction. His poetry, fiction and non-fiction have been published widely in literary magazines around the world and translated into Italian, Spanish, Serbian, Slovenian and

Portuguese. His latest work, *Trust the Bluer Skies* was published in 2024 by the University of Regina Press.

Arvee Fantilagan

Arvee Fantilagan grew up in the Philippines, lives in Japan, and has more of his works at sites.google.com/view/arveef. He hopes to write a better bio someday.

Christa Bedwin

Christa grew up in the Kananaskis among trees, rocks, wild things, big sky, and mysteries. She was 30 before she knew that her version of "a little strange" wasn't just isolation and an unusual upbringing but neurodivergence. What an enormous relief to realize there were others the same! Life has been better ever since. She likes math, sunshine, true words, doing her best, and being kind to as many people as possible. After many fairly solitary years as an editor and single mom, she has headed back high school teaching in remote Canada for a grand adventure.

Meghan Victoria

Meghan Victoria grew up in the northern wilds of Labrador and is obsessed with historical east coast life, all things weird and fantastic, yoga, and travel. She now lives in Calgary, Alberta with her husband and fat cat, Nancy. Her short fiction has been featured by a variety of publishers, including Radical Bookshop & Press, the Antigonish Review, and Coffin Hop Press. Meghan has spent two years as part of the Banff Centre Residency Program and currently teaches creative writing classes at the Alexandra Writers Centre Society.

Jason Ellis

Jason Ellis is a Kentucky writer. He and his family live on a farm with their horses, goats, dogs, cats, guinea pigs, and rats.

Nik Kuipers

Niki is a writer and amateur astrologer with an interest in all things occult.

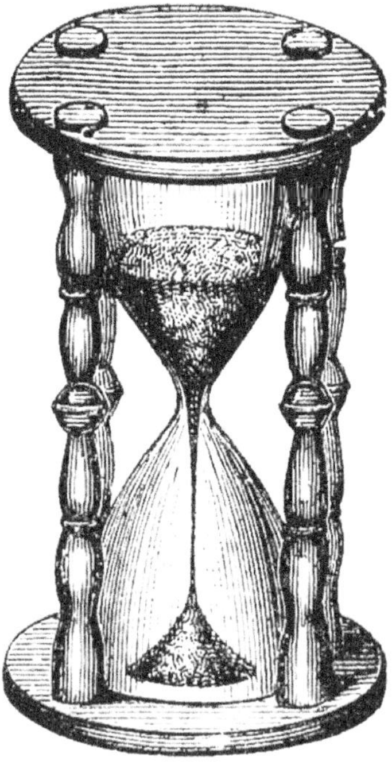

Copyrights

In the Hollow
© 2024 Cordelia Kelly

The Dragonfly
© 2024 Margaret Campbell

Mudge
© 2024 Kim Claussen

Rust for Rot
© 2024 Lareina Abbott

The Little Mushroom Girl
© 2024 Calvin D. Jim

Ruby Tips to Her Feathers
© 2024 Ash Vale

The Crone
© 2024 J.A. Renwick

Persephone, Queen of —I Don't Know—Some Bugs
© 2024 Alex Benarzi

The Moon & The Stars
© 2024 Joseph Halden & Rhonda Parrish

Extinction Burst
© 2024 Robert Fields Byrne

Forest Magic
© 2024 Valerie Hunter

A Mountain's Plea
© 2024 Andy Joe McCutchen

Roadkill Rising
© 2024 Brent Nichols

The Eerie Wood
© 2024 Emily A. Grigsby

The Intelligence
© 2024 paulo da costa

The Surprise Entrant
© 2024 Arvee Fantilagan

Amber & Jet
© 2024 Christa Bedwin

No Matter the Cost
© 2024 Meghan Victoria

Dirty Girl
© 2024 Sarah Johnson

Sacrifices
© 2024 Jason Ellis

Seasons
© 2024 Nik Kuipers

More

For more, go to ThePrairieSoul.com/press
PRAIRIE SOUL PRESS

Printed by Amazon Italia Logistica S.r.l.
Torrazza Piemonte (TO), Italy